Edgar Wallace was born illegitimately in 1875 in Greenwich and adopted by George Freeman, a porter at Billingsgate fish market. At eleven, Wallace sold newspapers at Ludgate Circus and on leaving school took a job with a printer. He enlisted in the Royal West Kent Regiment, later transferring to the Medical Staff Corps, and was sent to South Africa. In 1898 he published a collection of poems called *The Mission that Failed*, left the army and became a correspondent for Reuters.

Wallace became the South African war correspondent for *The ʼaily Mail*. His articles were later published as *Unofficial Dispatches* and is outspokenness infuriated Kitchener, who banned him as a war correspondent until the First World War. He edited the *Rand Daily Mail*, but gambled disastrously on the South African Stock Market, returning to England to report on crimes and hanging trials. He became editor of *The Evening News*, then in 1905 founded the Tallis Press, publishing *Smithy*, a collection of soldier stories, and *Four Just Men*. At various times he worked on *The Standard*, *The Star*, *The Week-End Racing Supplement* and *The Story Journal*.

In 1917 he became a Special Constable at Lincoln's Inn and also a special interrogator for the War Office. His first marriage to Ivy Caldecott, daughter of a missionary, had ended in divorce and he married his much younger secretary, Violet King.

The Daily Mail sent Wallace to investigate atrocities in the Belgian Congo, a trip that provided material for his *Sanders of the River* books. In 1923 he became Chairman of the Press Club and in 1931 stood as a Liberal candidate at Blackpool. On being offered a scriptwriting contract at RKO, Wallace went to Hollywood. He died in 1932, on his way to work on the screenplay for *King Kong*.

BY THE SAME AUTHOR
ALL PUBLISHED BY HOUSE OF STRATUS

The Just Men
of Cordova

HOUSE OF
STRATUS

as Executor of Mrs Margaret Penelope June Halcrow otherwise Penelope Wallace.

This edition published in 2001 by House of Stratus, an imprint of House of Stratus Ltd, Thirsk Industrial Park, York Road, Thirsk, North Yorkshire, YO7 3BX, UK.

www.houseofstratus.com

Typeset by House of Stratus, printed and bound by Short Run Press Limited.

A catalogue record for this book is available from the British Library and the Library of Congress.

ISBN 1-84232-691-0

We would like to thank the Edgar Wallace Society for all the support they have given House of Stratus. Enquiries on how to join the Edgar Wallace Society should be addressed to: The Edgar Wallace Society, c/o Penny Wyrd, 84 Ridgefield Road, Oxford, OX4 3DA. Email: info@edgarwallace.org Web: http://www.edgarwallace.org/

CONTENTS

THREE MEN OF CORDOVA

The man who sat at the marble-topped table of the Café of the Great Captain – if I translate the sign aright – was a man of leisure. A tall man, with a trim beard and grave grey eyes that searched the street absently as though not quite certain of his quest. He sipped a coffee *con leche* and drummed a little tune on the table with his slender white hands.

He was dressed in black, which is the conventional garb in Spain, and his black cloak was lined with velvet. His cravat was of black satin, and his well-fitting trousers were strapped under his pointed boots, in the manner affected by certain *caballero*.

These features of his attire were the most striking, though he was dressed conventionally enough – for Cordova. He might have been a Spaniard, for grey eyes are a legacy of the Army of Occupation, and many were the unions between Wellington's rollicking Irishmen and the susceptible ladies of the Estremadura.

His speech was flawless. He spoke with the lisp of Andalusia, clipping his words as do the folk of the South. Also, there was evidence of his Southern origin in his response to the whining beggar that shuffled painfully to him, holding out crooked fingers for largess.

"In the name of the Virgin, and the Saints, and the God who is above all, I beseech you, señor, to spare me ten centimos."

The bearded man brought his far-seeing eyes to focus on the palm.

"God will provide," he said, in the slurred Arabic of Spanish Morocco.

"Though I live a hundred years," said the beggar monotonously, "I will never cease to pray for your lordship's happiness."

He of the velvet-lined cloak looked at the beggar.

The mendicant was a man of medium height, sharp-featured, unshaven, after the way of his kind, terribly bandaged across his head and one eye.

Moreover, he was lame. His feet were shapeless masses of swathed bandages, and his discoloured hands clutched a stick fiercely.

"Señor and Prince," he whined, "there is between me and the damnable pangs of hunger ten centimos, and your worship would not sleep this night in comfort thinking of me tossing in famine."

"Go in peace," said the other patiently. "Exalted," moaned the beggar, "by the *chico* that lay on your mother's knee" – he crossed himself – "by the gallery of the Saints and the blessed blood of martyrs, I beseech you not to leave me to die by the wayside, when ten centimos, which is as the paring of your nails, would lead me to a full stomach."

The man at the table sipped his coffee unmoved.

"Go with God," he said.

Still the man lingered.

He looked helplessly up and down the sunlit street. He peered into the cool dark recess of the café, where an apathetic waiter sat at a table reading the *Heraldo*.

Then he leant forward, stretching out a slow hand to pick a crumb of cake from the next table.

"Do you know Dr Essley?" he asked in perfect English.

The cavalier at the table looked thoughtful. "I do not know him. Why?" he asked in the same language.

"You should know him," said the beggar; "he is interesting."

He said no more, shuffling a painful progress along the street. The *caballero* watched him with some curiosity as he made his way slowly to the next café.

Then he clapped his hands sharply, and the apathetic waiter, now nodding significantly over his *Heraldo*, came suddenly to life, collected the bill, and a tip which was in proportion to the size of the bill.

Though the sky was cloudless and the sun threw blue shadows in the street, those same shadows were immensely cold, for these were the chilly days before the first heat of spring.

The gentleman, standing up to his full height – he was well over the six-feet mark – shook his cloak and lightly threw one end across his shoulder; then he began to walk slowly in the direction taken by the beggar.

The way led him through narrow streets, so narrow that in the walls on either side ran deep recesses to allow the boxes of cartwheels to pass. He overtook the man in the Calle Paraiso, passed him, threading the narrow streets that led to San Fernando. Down this he went, walking very leisurely, then turned to the street of Carrera de Puente, and so came to the shadows of the mosque-cathedral which is dedicated to God and to Allah with delightful impartiality. He stood irresolutely before the gates that opened on to the courtyards, seemed half in doubt, then turned again, going downhill to the Bridge of Calahorra. Straight as a die the bridge runs, with its sixteen arches that the ancient Moors built. The man with the cloak reached the centre of the bridge and leant over, watching with idle interest the swollen yellow waters of the Guadalquivir.

Out of the corner of his eye he watched the beggar come slowly through the gate and walk in his direction. He had a long time to wait, for the man's progress was slow. At last he came sidling up to him, hat in hand, palm outstretched. The attitude was that of a beggar, but the voice was that of an educated Englishman.

"Manfred," he said earnestly, "you must see this man Essley. I have a special reason for asking."

"What is he?"

The beggar smiled.

"I am dependent upon memory to a great extent," he said, "the library at my humble lodgings being somewhat limited, but I have a dim idea that he is a doctor in a suburb of London, rather a clever surgeon."

"What is he doing here?"

The redoubtable Gonsalez smiled again.

3

"There is in Cordova a Dr Cajalos. From the exalted atmosphere of the Paseo de Gran Capitan, wherein I understand you have your luxurious suite, no echo of the underworld of Cordova comes to you. Here" – he pointed to the roofs and the untidy jumble of buildings at the farther end of the bridge – "in the Campo of the Verdad, where men live happily on two pesetas a week, we know Dr Cajalos. He is a household word – a marvellous man, George, performing miracles undreamt of in your philosophy: making the blind to see, casting spells upon the guilty, and creating infallible love philtres for the innocent! He'll charm a wart or arrest the ravages of sleeping sickness."

Manfred nodded.

"Even in the Paseo de la Gran Capitan he is not without honour," he said with a twinkle in his eye. "I have seen him and consulted him."

The beggar was a little astonished.

"You're a wonderful man," he said, with admiration in his voice. "When did you do it?"

Manfred laughed softly.

"There was a certain night, not many weeks ago, when a beggar stood outside the worthy doctor's door, patiently waiting till a mysterious visitor, cloaked to his nose, had finished his business."

"I remember," said the other, nodding. "He was a stranger from Ronda, and I was curious – did you see me following him?"

"I saw you," said Manfred gravely. "I saw you from the corner of my eye."

"It was not you?" asked Gonsalez, astonished.

"It was I," said the other. "I went out of Cordova to come into Cordova."

Gonsalez was silent for a moment.

"I accept the humiliation," he said. "Now, since you know the doctor, can you see any reason for the visit of a commonplace English doctor to Cordova? He has come all the way without a halt from England by the Algeciras Express. He leaves Cordova tomorrow morning at daybreak by the same urgent system, and he comes to consult Dr Cajalos."

"Poiccart is here: he has an interest in this Essley – so great an interest that he comes blandly to our Cordova, Baedeker in hand, seeking information of the itinerant guide and submitting meekly to his inaccuracies."

Manfred stroked his little beard, with the same grave thoughtful expression in his wise eyes as when he had watched Gonsalez shuffling from the Café de la Gran Capitan.

"Life would be dull without Poiccart," he said.

"Dull, indeed – ah, señor, my life shall be your praise, and it shall rise like the smoke of holy incense to the throne of Heaven."

He dropped suddenly into his whine, for a policeman of the town guard was approaching, with a suspicious eye for the beggar who stood with expectant hand outstretched.

Manfred shook his head as the policeman strolled up.

"Go in peace," he said.

"Dog," said the policeman, his rough hand descending on the beggar's shoulder, "thief of a thief, begone lest you offend the nostrils of this illustrious."

With arms akimbo, he watched the man limp away, then he turned to Manfred.

"If I had seen this scum before, excellency," he said fiercely, "I should have relieved your presence of his company."

"It is not important," said Manfred conventionally.

"As for me," the policeman went on, releasing one hand from his hip to curl an insignificant moustache, "I have hard work in protecting rich and munificent *caballeros* from these swine. And God knows my pay is poor, and with three hungry mouths to fill, not counting my wife's mother, who comes regularly on feast days and must be taken to the bull-fight, life is hard. More especially, señor, since she is one of those damned proud Andalusian women who must have a seat in the shade* at two pesetas. For myself, I have not tasted *rioja* since the feast of Santa Therese – "

---

* At a bull-fight the seats in the sun are the cheaper, those in the shade being double the price.

Manfred slipped a peseta into the hand of the uniformed beggar.

The man walked by his side to the end of the bridge, retailing his domestic difficulties with the freedom and intimacy which is possible nowhere else in the world. They stood chattering near the principal entrance to the Cathedral.

"Your excellency is not of Cordova?" asked the officer.

"I am of Malaga," said Manfred without hesitation.

"I had a sister who married a fisherman of Malaga," confided the policeman. "Her husband was drowned, and she now lives with a señor whose name I forget. She is a pious woman, but very selfish. Has your excellency been to Gibraltar?"

Manfred nodded. He was interested in a party of tourists which was being shown the glories of the Puerta del Perdon.

One of the tourists detached himself from his party and came towards them. He was a man of middle height and strongly built. There was a strange reserve in his air and a saturnine imperturbability in his face.

"Can you direct me to the Passeo de la Gran Capitan?" he asked in bad Spanish.

"I am going that way," said Manfred courteously; "if the señor would condescend to accompany me – "

"I shall be grateful," said the other.

They chatted a little on divers subjects – the weather, the delightful character of the mosque-cathedral.

"You must come along and see Essley," said the tourist suddenly. He spoke in perfect Spanish.

"Tell me about him," said Manfred. "Between you and Gonsalez, my dear Poiccart, you have piqued my curiosity."

"This is an important matter," said the other earnestly. "Essley is a doctor in a suburb of London. I have had him under observation for some months. He has a small practice – quite a little one – and he attends a few cases. Apparently he does no serious work in his suburb, and his history is a strange one. He was a student at University College, London, and soon after getting his degree left with a youth named Henley for Australia. Henley had been a hopeless failure and

6

had been badly ploughed in his exams, but the two were fast friends, which may account for their going away together to try their luck in a new country. Neither of them had a relation in the world, except Henley, who had a rich uncle settled somewhere in Canada, and whom he had never seen. Arrived in Melbourne, the two started off up country with some idea of making for the new gold diggings, which were in full swing at that time. I don't know where the diggings were; at any rate, it was three months before Essley arrived – alone, his companion having died on the road!"

"He does not seem to have started practising," Poiccart went on, "for three or four years. We can trace his wanderings from mining camp to mining camp, where he dug a little, gambled a lot, and was generally known as Dr S. – probably an abbreviation of Essley. Not until he reached Western Australia did he attempt to establish himself as a doctor. He had some sort of a practice, not a very high-class one, it is true, but certainly lucrative. He disappeared from Coolgardie in 1900; he did not reappear in England until 1908."

They had reached the Passeo by now. The streets were better filled than they had been when Manfred had followed the beggar.

"I've some rooms here," he said. "Come in and we will have some tea."

He occupied a flat over a jeweller's in the Calle Moreria. It was a well-furnished apartment, "and especially blessed in the matter of light," explained Manfred as he inserted the key. He put a silver kettle on the electric stove.

"The table is laid for two?" questioned Poiccart.

"I have visitors," said Manfred with a little smile. "Sometimes the begging profession becomes an intolerable burden to our Leon and he enters Cordova by rail, a most respectable member of society, full of a desire for the luxury of life – and stories. Go on with yours, Poiccart; I am interested."

The "tourist" seated himself in a deep arm-chair.

"Where was I?" he asked. "Oh, yes, Dr Essley disappeared from Coolgardie, and after an obliteration of eight years reappeared in London."

"In any exceptional circumstances?"

"No, very ordinarily. He seems to have been taken up by the newest kind of Napoleon."

"A Colonel Black?" asked Manfred, raising his eyebrows.

Poiccart nodded.

"That same meteor," he said. "At any rate, Essley, thanks to what practice he could steal from other practitioners in his own suburb – somewhere in the neighbourhood of Forest Hill – and what practice Napoleon's recommendation gives him, seems to be fairly well off. He first attracted my attention – "

There came a tap at the door, and Manfred raised his finger warningly. He crossed the room and opened the door. The concierge stood outside, cap in hand; behind him and a little way down the stairs was a stranger – obviously an Englishman.

"A señor to see your excellency," said the concierge.

"My house is at your disposal," said Manfred, addressing the stranger in Spanish.

"I am afraid I do not speak good Spanish," said the man on the stairs.

"Will you come up?" asked Manfred, in English.

The other mounted the stairs slowly.

He was a man of fifty. His hair was grey and long. His eyebrows were shaggy, and his under-jaw stuck out and gave his face an appearance which was slightly repulsive. He wore a black coat and carried a big, soft wideawake in his gloved hand.

He peered round the room from one to the other.

"My name," he said, "is Essley."

He pronounced the word, lingering upon the double "ss" till it sounded like a long hiss.

"Essley," he repeated as though he derived some satisfaction from the repetition – "Dr Essley."

Manfred motioned him to a chair, but he shook his head.

"I'll stand," he said harshly. "When I have business, I stand."

He looked suspiciously at Poiccart.

"I have private business," he said pointedly.

"My friend has my complete confidence," said Manfred.

He nodded grudgingly.

"I understand," he said, "that you are a scientist and a man of considerable knowledge of Spain."

Manfred shrugged his shoulders. In his present role he enjoyed some reputation as a quasi-scientific *littérateur*, and under the name of "de la Monte" had published a book on *Modern Crime*.

"Knowing this," said the man, "I came to Cordova, having other business also – but that will keep."

He looked round for a chair and Manfred offered one, into which he sat, keeping his back to the window.

"Mr de la Monte," said the doctor, leaning forward with his hands on his knees and speaking very deliberately, "you have some knowledge of crime."

"I have written a book on the subject," said Manfred, "which is not necessarily the same thing."

"I had that fear," said the other bluntly. "I was also afraid that you might not speak English. Now I want to ask you a plain question and I want a plain answer."

"So far as I can give you this, I shall be most willing," said Manfred.

The doctor twisted his face nervously, then – "Have you ever heard of the 'Four Just Men'?" he asked.

There was a little silence.

"Yes," said Manfred calmly, "I have heard of them."

"Are they in Spain?"

The question was put sharply.

"I have no exact knowledge," said Manfred. "Why do you ask?"

"Because – "The doctor hesitated. "Oh, well – I am interested. It is said that they unearth villainy that the law does not punish; they – they kill – eh?"

His voice was sharper, his eyelids narrowed till he peered from one to the other through slits.

"Such an organization is known to exist," said Manfred, "and one knows that they do hap upon unpunished crime – and punish."

"Even to – to killing?"

9

"They even kill," said Manfred gravely.

"And they go free!" – the doctor leapt to his feet with a snarl and flung out his hands in protest – "they go free! All the laws of all nations cannot trap them! A self-appointed tribunal – who are *they* to judge and condemn? Who gave *them* the right to sit in judgement? There is a law, if a man cheats it – "

He checked himself suddenly, shook his shoulders and sank heavily into the chair again.

"So far as I can secure information upon the subject," he said roughly, "these men are no longer an active force – they are outlawed – there are warrants for them in every country."

Manfred nodded.

"That is very true," he said gently; "but whether they are an active force, time must reveal."

"There were three?" – the doctor looked up quickly – "and they usually find a fourth – an influential fourth."

Manfred nodded again.

"So I understand."

Dr Essley twisted uncomfortably in his chair. It was evident that the information or assurance he expected to receive from this expert in crime was not entirely satisfactory to him.

"And they are in Spain?" he asked.

"So it is said."

"They are not in France; they are not in Italy; they are not in Russia; nor in any of the German States," said the doctor resentfully. "They must be in Spain."

He brooded awhile in silence.

"Pardon me," said Poiccart, who had been a silent listener, "but you seem very interested in these men. Would it be offensive to you if I asked you to satisfy my curiosity as to why you should be anxious to discover their whereabouts?"

"Curiosity also," said the other quickly; "in a sense I am a modest student of crime, as our friend de la Monte is."

"An enthusiastic student," said Manfred quietly.

"I hoped that you would be able to give me some help," Essley went on, unmindful of the significant emphasis of the other's tones; "beyond the fact that they may be in Spain, which, after all, is conjectural, I have learnt nothing."

"They may not even be in Spain," said Manfred, as he accompanied his visitor to the door; "they may not even be in existence – your fears may be entirely groundless."

The doctor whipped round, white to the lips "Fears?" he said, breathing quickly. "Did you say fears?"

"I am sorry," laughed Manfred easily; "my English is perhaps not good."

"Why should I fear them?" demanded the doctor aggressively. "Why should I? Your words are chosen very unwisely, sir. I have nothing to fear from the 'Four Just Men' – or from any other source."

He stood panting in the doorway like a man who is suddenly deprived of breath.

With an effort he collected himself, hesitated a moment, and then with a stiff little bow left the room.

He went down the stairs, out to the street, and turned into the Passeo.

There was a beggar at the corner who raised a languid hand.

"Por deos – ," he whined.

With an oath, Essley struck at the hand with his cane, only to miss it, for the beggar was singularly quick and, for all the discomforts he was prepared to face, Gonsalez had no desire to endure a hand seamed and wealed – those sensitive hands of his were assets to Gonsalez.

The doctor pursued a savage way to his hotel.

Reaching his room, he locked the door and threw himself into a chair to think. He cursed his own folly – it was madness to have lost his temper even before so insignificant a person as a Spanish dilettante in science.

There was the first half of his mission finished – and it was a failure. He took from the pocket of his overcoat, hanging behind the door, a

Spanish Baedeker. He turned the leaves till he came to a map of Cordova. Attached to this was a smaller plan, evidently made by somebody who knew the topography of the place better than he understood the rules of cartography.

He had heard of Dr Cajalos first from a Spanish anarchist he had met in some of his curious nocturnal prowlings in London. Under the influence of good wine this bold fellow had invested the wizard of Cordova with something approaching miraculous powers – he had also said things which had aroused the doctor's interest to an extraordinary degree. A correspondence had followed: the visit was the result.

Essley looked at his watch. It was nearly seven o'clock. He would dine, then go to his room and change.

He made a hasty ablution in the growing darkness of the room – curiously enough he did not switch on the light; then he went to dinner.

He had a table to himself and buried himself in an English magazine he had brought with him. Now and again as he read he would make notes in a little book which lay on the table by the side of his plate.

They had no reference to the article he read; they had little association with medical science. On the whole, they dealt with certain financial aspects of a certain problem which came into his mind.

He finished his dinner, taking his coffee at the table. Then he rose, put the little notebook in his pocket, the magazine under his arm, and made his way back to his room. He turned on the light, pulled down the blinds, and drew a light dressing-table beneath the lamp. He produced his note-book again and, with the aid of a number of closely written sheets of paper taken from his valise, he compiled a little table. He was completely engrossed for a couple of hours. As if some invisible and unheard alarm clock warned him of his engagement, he closed the book, locked his memoranda in the valise, and struggled into his coat. With a soft felt hat pulled down over his eyes, he left the hotel and without hesitation took the path which led down to the

Calahorra Bridge. The streets through which he passed were deserted, but he had no hesitation, knowing well the lawful character of these unprepossessing little Spanish suburbs.

He plunged into a labyrinth of narrow streets – he had studied his plan to some purpose – and only hesitated when he reached a cul-de-sac which was more spacious than the street from which it opened. One oil lamp at the farther end added rather to the gloom. Tall, windowless houses rose on either side, and each was pierced by a door. On the left door the doctor, after a moment's hesitation, knocked twice.

Instantly it opened noiselessly. He hesitated.

"Enter," said a voice in Spanish; "the señor need not fear."

He stepped into the black void and the door closed behind him.

"Come this way," said the voice. In the pitch darkness he could make out the indistinct figure of a little man.

The doctor stepped inside and surreptitiously wiped the sweat from his forehead. The old man lit a lamp, and Essley took stock of him. He was very little, scarcely more than four feet in height. He had a rough white beard and head as bald as an egg. His face and hands were alike grimy, and his whole appearance bore evidence of his aversion to water.

A pair of black twinkling eyes were set deeply in his head, and the puckering lines about them revealed him as a man who found humour in life. This was Dr Cajalos, a famous man in Spain, though he had no social standing.

"Sit down," said Cajalos; "we will talk quietly, for I have a señora of high quality to see me touching a matter of lost affection."

Essley took the chair offered to him and the doctor seated himself on a high stool by the table. A curious figure he made, with his dangling little legs, his old, old face and his shining bald pate.

"I wrote to you on the subject of certain occult demonstrations," began the doctor, but the old man stopped him with a quick jerk of the hand.

"You came to see me, señor, because of a drug I have prepared," he said, "a preparation of – " ★

Essley sprang to his feet.

"I – I did not tell you so," he stammered. "The green devil told me," said the other seriously. "I have many talks with the foot-draggers, and they speak very truly."

"I thought – "

"Look!" said the old man.

He leapt down from his high perch with agility. In the dark corner of one of the rooms were some boxes, to which he went. Essley heard a scuffling, and by and by the old man came back, holding by the ears a wriggling rabbit.

With his disengaged hand he unstoppered a little green bottle on the table. He picked a feather from the table, dipped the point gingerly into the bottle. Then very carefully he lightly touched the nose of the rabbit with the end of the feather – so lightly, indeed, that the feather hardly brushed the muzzle of the animal.

Instantly, with no struggle, the rabbit went limp, as though the life essence had been withdrawn from the body. Cajalos replaced the stopper and thrust the feather into a little charcoal fire that burnt dully in the centre of the room.

"P–e," he said briefly; "but my preparation."

He laid the dead animal on the floor at the feet of the other.

"Señor," he said proudly, "you shall take that animal and examine it; you shall submit it to tests beyond patience; yet you shall not discover the alkaloid that killed it."

"That is not so," said Essley, "for there will be a contraction of the pupil which is an invariable sign."

"Search also for that," said the old man triumphantly.

★ In the story, as it appeared in serial form, the name of the poison occurred. It has been represented to the author (and he agrees) that it is wholly undesirable that the name of this drug should appear in a work of fiction. It is one well known to oculists and its action is faithfully described in these pages.

Essley made the superficial tests. There was not even this invariable symptom.

A dark figure, pressed close to the wall outside, listened. He was standing by the shuttered window. He held to his ear a little ebonite tube with a microphonic receiver, and the rubber which covered the bell-like end was pressed against the shutter.

For half an hour he stood thus, almost motionless, then he withdrew silently and disappeared into the shadows of the orange grove that grew in the centre of the long garden.

As he did so, the door of the house opened and, with lantern in hand, Cajalos showed his visitor into the street.

"The devils are greener than ever," chuckled the old man. "Hey! there will be happenings, my brother!"

Essley said nothing. He wanted to be in the street again. He stood quivering with nervous impatience as the old man unfastened the heavy door, and when it swung open he almost leapt into the street outside.

"Goodbye," he said.

"Go with God," said the old man, and the door closed noiselessly.

COLONEL BLACK, FINANCIER

The firm of Black and Gram had something of a reputation in City circles. Gram might have been a man beyond reproach – a veritable Bayard of finance, a churchgoer, and a generous subscriber to charities. Indeed, Black complained with good-humoured irritation – if the combination can be visualized – that Gram would ruin him one of these fine days by his quixotic munificence.

Gram allowed his heart to dictate to his head; he was too soft for business, too retiring. The City was very sceptical about Gram. It compared him with a certain Mrs Harris, but Black did not fly into a temper; he smiled mysteriously at all the suspicion which the City entertained or expressed, and went on deploring the criminal rustiness of a man who apparently sought, by Black's account, to made the firm reputable in spite of the rumours which centred about Colonel J Black.

In this way did Black describe himself, though the Army list was innocent of his name, and even a search through the voluminous rolls of the American honorary ranks failed to reveal any association.

Black and Gram floated companies and dealt largely in stocks and shares. They recommended to their clients certain shares, and the clients bought or sold according to the advice given, and at the end of a certain period of time, Black and Gram wrote politely regretting that the cover deposited had been exhausted, and urgently requesting, with as little delay as possible, the discharge of those liabilities which in some extraordinary fashion the client had incurred. This, at any rate, was the humble beginnings of a firm which was destined to grow to important proportions. Gram went out of the business – was never in it, if the truth be told. One doubts if he ever breathed the breath of life – and Black grew in prosperity. His was a name to conjure with in certain circles. In others it was never mentioned. The financial lords of the City – the Farings, the Wertheiners, the Scott-Teasons – had no official knowledge of his existence. They went about their business calmly, loaning their millions at a ridiculously small percentage, issuing Government loans, discounting bills, buying bullion, and such-like operations which filled the hours between eleven o'clock, when their electric broughams set them down in Threadneedle Street, and four o'clock, when their electric broughams picked them up again.

They read of Colonel Black in their grave way, because there were days when he dominated the financial columns. They read of his mighty stock deals, of his Argentine electric deal, his rubber flotations and his Canadian copper mines. They read about him, neither approving nor disapproving. They regarded him with that dispassionate interest which a railway engine has for a motorcar.

When, on one never-to-be-forgotten occasion, he approached the financial lords with a promising proposition, they "regretted they were unable to entertain Colonel Black's interesting suggestion." A little baffled, a little annoyed, he approached the big American group, for it was necessary for the success of his scheme that there should be names on his prospectus. Shrewd fellows, these Americans, thought Colonel Black, and he set forth his proposals in terms which were at once immodest and alluring. In reply – "Dear friend" (it was one of those American businesses that turn down a million dollars with five cents' worth of friendship), "we have carefully considered your proposition, and whilst we are satisfied that you will make money by its fruition, we are not so certain that we shall."

Black came to the City of London one afternoon to attend a board of directors' meeting. He had been out of town for a few days, recruiting in advance, as he informed the board with a touch of facetiousness, for the struggle that awaited him.

He was a man of middle height, broad of shoulder. His face was thin and lank, his complexion sallow, with a curious uniform yellowness. If you saw Colonel Black once you would never forget him – not only because of that yellow face of his, that straight black bar of eyebrow and the thin-lipped mouth, but the very personality of the man impressed itself indelibly on the mind of the observer.

His manner was quick, almost abrupt; his replies brusque. A sense of finality marked his decisions. If the financial lords knew him not, there were thousands that did. His name was a household word in England. There was hardly a middle-class family that did not hold his stock. The little "street punters" hung on his word, his issues were subscribed for twice over. And he had established himself in five years; almost unknown before, he had risen to the dizziest heights in that short space of time.

Punctual to the minute, he entered the board-room of the suite of offices he occupied in Moorgate Street.

The meeting had threatened to be a stormy one. Again an amalgamation was in the air, and again the head of one group of ironmasters – it was an iron combine he was forming – had stood against the threats and blandishments of Black and his emissaries.

"The others are weakening," said Fanks, that big, hairless man; "you promised us that you would put him straight."

"I will keep my promise," said Black shortly.

"Widdison stood out, but he died," continued Fanks. "We can't expect Providence to help us all the time."

Black's eyebrows lowered.

"I do not like jests of that kind," he said. "Sandford is an obstinate man, a proud man; he needs delicate handling. Leave him to me."

The meeting adjourned lamely enough, and Black was leaving the room when Fanks beckoned to him.

"I met a man yesterday who knew your friend, Dr Essley, in Australia," he said.

"Indeed."

Colonel Black's face was expressionless.

"Yes – he knew him in his very early days – he was asking me where he could find him."

The other shrugged his shoulders. "Essley is abroad, I think – you don't like him?"

Augustus Fanks shook his head.

"I don't like doctors who come to see me in the middle of the night, who are never to be found when they are wanted, and are always jaunting off to the Continent."

"He is a busy man," excused Black. "By the way, where is your friend staying?"

"He isn't a friend, he's a sort of prospector, name of Weld, who has come to London with a mining proposition. He is staying at Varlet's Temperance Hotel in Bloomsbury."

"I will tell Essley when he returns," said Black, nodding his head.

He returned to his private office in a thoughtful mood. All was not well with Colonel Black. Reputedly a millionaire, he was in the position of many a financier who counted his wealth in paper. He had got so far climbing on the shadows. The substance was still beyond his reach. He had organized successful combinations, but the cost had been heavy. Millions had flowed through his hands, but precious little had stuck. He was that curious contradiction – a dishonest man with honest methods. His schemes were financially sound, yet it had needed almost superhuman efforts to get them through.

He was in the midst of an unpleasant reverie when a tap on the door aroused him. It opened to admit Fanks.

He frowned at the intruder, but the other pulled up a chair and sat down.

"Look here, Black," he said, "I want to say something to you."

"Say it quickly."

Fanks took a cigar from his pocket and lit it.

"You've had a marvellous career," he said. "I remember when you started with a little bucketshop – well, we won't call it a bucket shop," he said hastily as he saw the anger rising in the other's face, "outside broker's. You had a mug – I mean an inexperienced partner who found the money."

"Yes."

"Not the mysterious Gram, I think?"

"His successor – there was nothing mysterious about Gram."

"A successor named Flint?"

"Yes."

"He died unexpectedly, didn't he?"

"I believe he did," said Black abruptly. "Providence again," said Fanks slowly; "then you got the whole of the business. You took over the flotation and a rubber company, and it panned out. Well, after that you floated a tin mine or something – there was a death there, wasn't there?"

"I believe there was – one of the directors; I forget his name."

Fanks nodded.

"He could have stopped the flotation – he was threatening to resign and expose some methods of yours."

"He was a very headstrong man."

"And he died."

"Yes," – a pause – "he died."

Fanks looked at the man who sat opposite to him.

"Dr Essley attended him."

"I believe he did."

"And he died."

Black leant over the desk.

"What do you mean?" he asked. "What are you suggesting about my friend, Dr Essley?"

"Nothing, except that Providence has been of some assistance to you," said Fanks. "The record of your success is a record of death – you sent Essley to see me once."

"You were ill."

"I was," said Fanks grimly, "and I was also troubling you a little." He flicked the ash from his cigar to the carpet. "Black, I'm going to resign all my directorships on your companies."

The other man laughed unpleasantly.

"You can laugh, but it isn't healthy, Black. I've no use for money that is bought at too heavy a price."

"My dear man, you can resign," said Colonel Black, "but might I ask if your extraordinary suspicions are shared by anybody else?"

Fanks shook his head.

"Not at present," he said.

They looked at one another for the space of half a minute, which was a very long time.

"I want to clear right out," Fanks continued. "I reckon my holdings are worth £150,000 – you can buy them."

"You amaze me," said Black harshly.

He opened a drawer of his desk and took out a little green bottle and a feather.

"Poor Essley," he smiled, "wandering about Spain seeking the secrets of Moorish perfumery – he would go off his head if he knew what you thought of him."

"I'd sooner he went off his head than that I should go off the earth," said Fanks stolidly. "What have you got there?"

Black unstoppered the bottle and dipped in the feather.

He withdrew it and held it close to his nose.

"What is it?" asked Fanks curiously.

For answer, Black held up the feather for the man to smell.

"I can smell nothing," said Fanks.

Tilting the end quickly downwards, Black drew it across the lips of the other.

"Here…" cried Fanks, and went limply to the ground.

"Constable Fellowe!"

Frank Fellowe was leaving the charge-room when he heard the snappy tones of the desk sergeant calling him.

"Yes, sergeant?" he said, with a note of inquiry in his voice. He knew that there was something unpleasant coming.

Sergeant Gurden seldom took any opportunity of speaking to him, except in admonishment. The sergeant was a wizen-faced man, with an ugly trick of showing his teeth when he was annoyed, and no greater contrast could be imagined than that which was afforded by the tall, straight-backed young man in the constable's uniform, standing before the desk, and the shrunken figure that sat on the stool behind.

Sergeant Gurden had a dead-white face, which a scrubby black moustache went to emphasize. In spite of the fact that he was a man of good physical development, his clothing hung upon him awkwardly, and indeed the station-sergeant was awkward in more ways than one.

Now he looked at Fellowe, showing his teeth.

"I have had another complaint about you," he said, "and if this is repeated it will be a matter for the Commissioner."

The constable nodded his head respectfully.

"I am very sorry, sergeant," he said, "but what is the complaint?"

"You know as well as I do," snarled the other; "you have been annoying Colonel Black again."

A faint smile passed across Fellowe's lips. He knew something of the solicitude in which the sergeant held the colonel.

"What the devil are you smiling at?" snapped the sergeant. "I warn you," he went on, "that you are getting very impertinent, and this may be a matter for the Commissioner."

"I had no intention of being disrespectful, sergeant," said the young man. "I am as tired of these complaints as you are, but I have told you, as I will tell the Commissioner, that Colonel Black lives in a house in Serrington Gardens and is a source of some interest to me – that is my excuse."

"He complains that you are always watching the house," said the sergeant, and Constable Fellowe smiled.

"That is his conscience working," he said. "Seriously, sergeant, I happen to know that the colonel is not too friendly disposed – "

He stopped himself.

"Well?" demanded the sergeant.

"Well," repeated Constable Fellowe, "it might be as well perhaps if I kept my thoughts to myself."

The sergeant nodded grimly.

"If you get into trouble you will only have yourself to blame," he warned. "Colonel Black is an influential man. He is a ratepayer. Don't forget that, constable. The ratepayers pay your salary, find the coat for your back, feed you – you owe everything to the ratepayers."

"On the other hand," said the young man, "Colonel Black is a ratepayer who owes me something."

Hitching his cape over his arm, he passed from the charge-room down the stone steps into the street without.

The man on duty at the door bade him a cheery farewell.

Fellowe was an annoying young man, more annoying by reason of the important fact that his antecedents were quite unknown to his most intimate friends. He was a man of more than ordinary education, quiet, restrained, his voice gently modulated; he had all the manners and attributes of a gentleman.

He had a tiny little house in Somers Town where he lived alone, but no friend of his, calling casually, had ever the good fortune to find him at home when he was off duty. It was believed he had other interests.

What those interests were could be guessed when, with exasperating unexpectedness, he appeared in the amateur boxing championship and carried off the police prize, for Fellowe was a magnificent boxer – hard hitting, quick, reliable, scientific.

The bad men of Somers Town were the first to discover this, and one, Grueler, who on one never-to-be-forgotten occasion had shown fight on the way to the station, testified before breathless audiences as to the skill and science of the young man.

His breezy independence had won for him many friends, but it had made him enemies too, and as he walked thoughtfully along the street leading from the station, he realized that in the sergeant he had an enemy of more than average malignity.

Why should this be? It puzzled him. After all, he was only doing his duty. That he was also exceeding his duty did not strike him as being sufficient justification for the resentment of his superior, for he had reached the enthusiastic age of life where only inaction was unpardonable. As to Black, Frank shrugged his shoulders. He could not understand it. He was not of a nature to suspect that the sergeant had any other motive than the perfectly natural desire which all blasé superiors have, to check their too impulsive subordinates.

Frank admitted to himself that he was indeed a most annoying person, and in many ways he understood the sergeant's antagonism to himself. Dismissing the matter from his mind, he made his way to his tiny house in Croome Street and let himself into his small dining-room.

The walls were distempered, and the few articles of furniture that were within were such as are not usually met with in houses of this quality. The old print above the mantelpiece must have been worth a workingman's annual income. The small gate-legged table in the centre of the felt-covered floor was indubitably Jacobean, and the chairs were Sheraton, as also was the sideboard.

Though the periods may not have harmonized, there is harmony enough in great age. A bright fire was burning in the grate, for the night was bitterly cold. Fellowe stopped before the mantelpiece to examine two letters which stood awaiting him, replaced them from where he had taken them, and passed through the folding doors of the room into a tiny bedroom.

He had an accommodating landlord. Property owners in Somers Town, and especially the owners of small cottages standing on fairly valuable ground, do not as a rule make such renovations as Fellowe required. The average landlord, for instance, would not have built the spacious bathroom which the cottage boasted, but then Fellowe's landlord was no ordinary man.

The young man bathed, changed himself into civilian clothing, made himself a cup of tea, and, slipping into a long overcoat which reached to his heels, left the house half an hour after he had entered.

Frank Fellowe made his way West. He found a taxi-cab at King's Cross and gave an address in Piccadilly. Before he had reached that historic thoroughfare he tapped at the window-glass and ordered the cabman to drop him.

At eleven o'clock that night Sergeant Gurden, relieved from his duty, left the stationhouse. Though outwardly taciturn and calm, he was boiling internally with wrath.

His antipathy to Fellowe was a natural one, but it had become intensified during the past few weeks by the attitude which the young man had taken up towards the sergeant's protégé.

Gurden was as much of a mystery to the men in his division as Fellowe, and even more so, because the secrecy which surrounded Gurden's life had a more sinister import than the reservation of the younger man.

Gurden was cursed with an ambition. He had hoped at the outset of his career to have secured distinction in the force, but a lack of education, coupled with an address which was apt to be uncouth and brusque, had militated against his enthusiasm.

He had recognized the limitations placed upon his powers by the authorities over him. He had long since come to realize that hope of promotion, first to an inspectorship, and eventually to that bright star which lures every policeman onward, and which is equivalent to the baton popularly supposed to be in every soldier's knapsack, a superintendentship, was not for him.

Thwarted ambition had to find a new outlet, and he concentrated his attention upon acquiring money. It became a passion for him, an obsession. His parsimony, his meanness, and his insatiable greed were bywords throughout the Metropolitan police force.

It had become a mania with him, this collecting of money, and his bitterest enmity was reserved for those who placed the slightest obstacle between the officer and the gratification of his ambitions.

It must be said of Colonel Black that he had been most kind. Cupidity takes a lenient view of its benefactor's morals, and though Sergeant Gurden was not the kind of man willingly to help the lawless, no person could say that an outside broker, undetected of fraud, was anything but a desirable member of society.

Black had made an appointment with him. He was on his way now to keep it. The colonel lived in one of those one-time fashionable squares in Camden Town. He was obviously well off, ran a car of his own, and had furnished No. 60 Serrington Gardens with something like lavish comfort.

The sergeant had no time to change. There was no necessity, he told himself, for his relations with Black were of such a character that there was no need to stand on ceremony.

The square was deserted at this time of night, and the sergeant made his way to the kitchen entrance in the basement and rang the bell.

The door was opened almost instantly by a man-servant.

"Is that you, sergeant?" said a voice from the darkness, as Gurden made his way upstairs to the unlighted hall above.

Colonel Black turned on the light. He held out a long muscular hand in welcome to the police officer.

"I am so glad you have come," he said. The sergeant took the hand and shook it warmly.

"I have come to apologize to you, Colonel Black," he said. "I have severely reprimanded Police Constable Fellowe."

Black waved his hand deprecatingly. "I do not wish to get any member of your admirable force into trouble," he said, "but really this man's prying into my business is inexcusable and humiliating."

The sergeant nodded.

"I can well understand your annoyance, sir," he said, "but you will understand that these young constables are always a little over-zealous, and when a man is that way he is inclined to overdo it a little."

He spoke almost pleadingly in his desire to remove any bad impression that might exist in Black's mind as to his own part in Police Constable Fellowe's investigations.

Black favoured him with a gracious bow.

"Please do not think of it, I beg of you," he said. "I am perfectly sure that the young constable did not intend willingly to hurt my amour-propre."

He led the way to a spacious dining-room situated at the back of the house. Whisky and cigars were on the table.

"Help yourself, sergeant," said Colonel Black. He pushed a big comfortable chair forward.

With a murmured word of thanks, the sergeant sank into its luxurious depths.

"I am due back at the station in half an hour," he said, "if you will excuse me then."

Black nodded.

"We shall be able to do our business in that time," he said, "but before we go any further, let me thank you for what you have already done."

From the inside pocket of his coat he took a flat pocket-book, opened it and extracted two banknotes. He laid them on the table at the sergeant's elbow.

The sergeant protested feebly, but his eyes twinkled at the sight of the crinkling paper.

"I don't think I have done anything to deserve this," he muttered.

Colonel Black smiled, and his big cigar tilted happily.

"I pay well for little services, sergeant," he said. "I have many enemies – men who will misrepresent my motives – and it is essential that I should be forewarned."

He strode up and down the apartment thoughtfully, his hands thrust into his trousers pockets.

"It is a hard country, England," he said, "for men who have had the misfortune to dabble in finance."

Sergeant Gurden murmured sympathetically.

"In our business, sergeant," the aggrieved colonel went on, "it frequently happens that disappointed people – people who have not made the profits which they anticipated – bring extraordinary accusations against those responsible for the conduct of those concerns in which their money is invested. I had a letter today" – he shrugged his shoulders – "accusing me – me! – of running a bucket shop."

The sergeant nodded; he could well understand that aspect of speculation.

"And one has friends," Black went on, striding up and down the apartment, "one has people one wants to protect against similar annoyances – take my friend Dr Essley – Essley, E double s l e y," he spelt the name carefully; "you have heard of him?"

The sergeant had not heard of any such body, but was willing to admit that he had.

"There is a man," said the colonel, "a man absolutely at the head of his profession – I shouldn't be surprised to learn that even he is no safer from the voice of slander."

The sergeant thought it very likely, and murmured to the effect.

"There is always a possibility that malignity will attach itself to the famous," the colonel continued, "and because I know that you would be one of the first to hear such slander, and that you would moreover afford me an opportunity – a private opportunity – of combating such slander, that I feel such security. God bless you, sergeant!" He patted the other's shoulder, and Gurden was genuinely affected.

"I can quite understand your position, sir," he said, "and you may be sure that when it is possible to render you any assistance I shall be most happy and proud to render it."

Again Colonel Black favoured his visitor with a little pat.

"Or to Dr Essley," he said; "remember the name.

"Now, sergeant," he went on, "I sent for you tonight" – he shrugged his shoulders – "when I say sent for you, that, of course, is an exaggeration. How can a humble citizen like myself command the services of an officer of the police?"

Sergeant Gurden fingered his moustache self-consciously.

"It is rather," the colonel went on, "that I take advantage of your inestimable friendship to seek your advice."

He stopped in his walk, drew a chair opposite to where the sergeant was sitting, and seated himself.

"Constable Fellowe, the man of whom I have complained, had the good fortune to render a service to the daughter of Mr Theodore Sandford – I see you know the gentleman."

The sergeant nodded; he had heard of Mr Theodore Sandford, as who had not? For Theodore Sandford was a millionaire ironmaster who had built a veritable palace at Hampstead, had purchased the Dennington "Velasquez," and had presented it to the nation.

"Your constable," continued Colonel Black, "sprang upon a motor-car Miss Sandford was driving down a steep hill, the brakes of which had gone wrong, and at some risk to himself guided the car through the traffic when, not to put too fine a point on it, Miss Sandford had lost her head."

"Oh, it was him, was it?" said the sergeant disparagingly.

"It was him," agreed the colonel out of sheer politeness. "Now these young people have met unknown to the father of Miss Sandford, and – well, you understand."

The sergeant did not understand, but said nothing.

"I do not suggest," said the colonel, "that there is anything wrong – but a policeman, sergeant, not even an officer like yourself – a policeman!"

Deplorable! said the sergeant's head, eyes and hands.

"For some extraordinary reason which I cannot fathom," the colonel proceeded, "Mr Sandford tolerates the visits of this young man; that, I fear, is a matter which we cannot go into, but I should like you – well, I should like you to use your influence with Fellowe."

Sergeant Gurden rose to depart. He had no influence, but some power. He understood a little of what the other man was driving at, the more so when – "If this young man gets into trouble, I should like to know," said Colonel Black, holding out his firm hand; "I should like to know very much indeed."

"He is a rare pushful fellow, that Fellowe," said the sergeant severely. "He gets to know the upper classes in some way that I can't understand, and I dare say he has wormed himself into their confidence. I always say that the kitchen is the place for the policeman, and when I see a constable in the drawing-room I begin to suspect things. There is a great deal of corruption – " He stopped, suddenly realizing that he himself was in a drawing-room, and that corruption was an ugly and an incongruous word.

Colonel Black accompanied him to the door. "You understand, sergeant," he said, "that this man – Fellowe, did you call him? – may make a report over your head or behind your back. I want you to take great care that such a report, if it is made, shall come to me. I do not want to be taken by surprise. If there is any charge to answer I want to know all about it in advance. It will make the answering ever so much easier, as I am a busy man."

He shook hands with the sergeant and saw him out of the house.

Sergeant Gurden went back to the station with a brisk step and a comforting knowledge that the evening had been well spent.

AN ADVENTURE IN PIMLICO

In the meantime our constable had reached a small tavern in the vicinity of Regent Street.

He entered the bar and, ordering a drink, took a seat in the corner of the spacious saloon. There were two or three people about; there were two or three men drinking at the bar and talking – men in loud suits, who cast furtive glances at every newcomer. He knew them to be commonplace criminals of the first type. They did not engage his attention: he flew higher.

He sat in the corner, apparently absorbed in an evening paper, with his whisky and soda before him scarcely touched, waiting.

It was not the first time he had been here, nor would it be the first time he had waited without any result. But he was patient and dogged in the pursuit of his object.

The clock pointed to a quarter after ten, when the swing-doors were pushed open and two men entered.

For the greater part of half an hour the two were engaged in a low-voiced consultation. Over his paper Frank could see the face of Sparks. He was the jackal of the Black gang, the man-of-all-trades. To him were deputed the meanest of Black's commissions, and worthily did he serve his master. The other was known to Frank as Jakobs, a common thief and a pensioner of the benevolent colonel.

The conversation was punctuated either by glances at the clock above the bar or at Sparks' watch, and at a quarter to eleven the two men rose and went out.

Frank followed, leaving his drink almost untouched.

The men turned into Regent Street, walked a little way up, and then hailed a taxi.

Another cab was passing. Frank beckoned it.

"Follow that yellow cab," he said to the driver, "and keep a reasonable distance behind, and when it sets down, pass it and drop me farther along the street."

The man touched his cap. The two cabs moved on.

They went in the direction of Victoria, passed the great station on the left, turned down Grosvenor Road on the right, and were soon in the labyrinth of streets that constitute Pimlico.

The first cab pulled up at a big, gaunt house in a street which had once been fashionable, but which now hovered indescribably between slums and shabby gentility.

Frank saw the two men get out, and descended himself a few hundred yards farther along on the opposite side of the street. He had marked the house. There was no difficulty in distinguishing it; a brass plate was attached to the door announcing it to be an employment agency – as, indeed, it was.

His quarry had entered before he strode across towards the house. He crossed the road and took a position from whence he could watch the door.

The half-hour after twelve had chimed from a neighbouring church before anything happened.

A policeman on his beat had passed Frank with a resentful sidelong glance, and the few pedestrians who were abroad at that hour viewed him with no less suspicion.

The chime of the neighbouring church had hardly died away when a private car came swiftly along the road and pulled up with a jerk in front of the house.

A man descended. From where he stood Frank had no difficulty in recognizing Black. That he was expected was evident from the fact that the door was immediately opened to him.

Three minutes later another car came down the street and stopped a few doors short of the house, as though the driver was not quite certain as to which was his destination.

The newcomer was a stranger to Frank. In the uncertain light cast by a street lamp he seemed to be fashionably dressed.

As he turned to give instructions to his chauffeur, Fellowe caught a glimpse of a spotless white shirt-front beneath the long dark overcoat.

He hesitated at the foot of the steps which led to the door, and ascended slowly and fumbled for a moment at the bell. Before he could touch it the door opened. There was a short parley as the new man entered.

Frank, waiting patiently on the other side of the road, saw a light appear suddenly on the first floor.

Did he but know, this gathering was in the nature of a board meeting, a board meeting of a company more heavily financed than some of the most respected houses in the City, having its branches in various parts of the world, its agents, its business system – its very books, if they could be found and the ciphered entries unravelled.

Black sat at one end of the long table and the last arrival at the other. He was a florid young man of twenty-six, with a weak chin and a slight yellow moustache. His face would be familiar to all racing men, for this was the sporting baronet, Sir Isaac Tramber.

There was something about Sir Isaac which kept him on the outside fringe of good society, in spite of the fact that he came of a stock which was indelibly associated with England's story: the baronetcy had been created as far back as the seventeenth century.

It was a proud name, and many of his ancestors had borne it proudly. None the less, his name was taboo, his invitations politely refused, and never reciprocated.

There had been some unfathomable scandal associated with his name. Society is very lenient to its children. There are crimes and sins which it readily, or if not readily, at any rate eventually, forgives and condones, but there are some which are unpardonable, unforgivable. Once let a man commit those crimes, or sin those sins, and the doors of Mayfair are closed for ever against him.

Around his head was a cloud of minor scandal, but that which brought down the bar of good society was the fact that he had ridden his own horse at one of the Midland meetings. It had started a hot favourite – five to two on.

The circumstances of that race are inscribed in the annals of the Jockey Club. How an infuriated mob broke down the barriers and attempted to reach this amateur jockey was ably visualized by the sporting journalists who witnessed the extraordinary affair.

Sir Isaac was brought before the local stewards and the case submitted to the stewards of the Jockey Club. The next issue of the *Racing Calendar* contained the ominous announcement that Sir Isaac Tramber had been "warned off" Newmarket Heath.

Under this ban he sat for four years, till the withdrawal of the notice.

He might again attend race-meetings and own horses, and he did both, but the ban of society, that unwritten "warning off" notice, had not been withdrawn.

The doors of every decent house were closed to him.

Only one friend he had in the fashionable world, and there were people who said that the Earl of Verlond, that old and crabbed and envenomed man, merely championed his unpromising protégé out of sheer perversity, and there was ample justification for this contention of a man who was known to have the bitterest tongue in Europe.

The descent to hell is proverbially easy, and Sir Isaac Tramber's descent was facilitated by that streak of decadence which had made itself apparent even in his early youth.

As he sat at one end of the board-table, both hands stuffed into his trousers pockets, his head on one side like a perky bird, he proved no mean man of business, as Black had discovered earlier in their acquaintanceship.

"We are all here now, I think," said Black, looking humorously at his companion. They had left Sparks and his friend in a room below.

"I have asked you to come tonight," he said, "to hear a report of this business. I am happy to tell you that we have made a bigger profit this year than we have ever made in the course of our existence."

He went on to give details of the work for which he had been responsible, and he did so with the air and in the manner of one who was addressing a crowded board-room.

"People would say," said the colonel oracularly, "that the business of outside broker is inconsistent with my acknowledged position in the world of finance; therefore I deem it expedient to dissociate myself from our little firm. But the outside broker is a useful person – especially the outside broker who has a hundred thousand clients. There are stocks of mine which he can recommend with every evidence of disinterestedness, and just now I am particularly desirous that these stocks should be recommended."

"Do we lose anything by Fanks' death?" asked the baronet carelessly. "Hard luck on him, wasn't it? But he was awfully fat."

The colonel regarded the questioner with a calm stare.

"Do not let us refer to Fanks," he said evenly. "The death of Fanks has very much upset me – I do not wish to speak about it."

The baronet nodded.

"I never trusted him, poor chap," he said, "any more than I trusted the other chap who made such an awful scene here a year ago – February, wasn't it?"

"Yes," said the colonel briefly.

"It's lucky for us he died too." said the tactless aristocrat, "because – "

"We'll get on with the business."

Colonel Black almost snarled the words.

But the baronet had something to say. He was troubled about his own security. It was when Black showed some sign of ending the business that Sir Isaac leant forward impatiently.

"There is one thing we haven't discussed, Black," he said.

Black knew what the thing was, and had carefully avoided mention of the subject.

"What is it?" he asked innocently.

"These fellows who are threatening us, or rather threatening you; they haven't any idea who it is who is running the show, have they?" he asked, with some apprehension.

Black shook his head smilingly.

"I think not," he said. "You are speaking, of course, of the 'Four Just Men.' "

Sir Isaac gave a short nod.

"Yes," Black went on, with an assumption of indifference, "I have had an anonymous letter from these gentlemen. As a matter of fact, my dear Sir Isaac, I haven't the slightest doubt that the whole thing is a bluff."

"What do you mean by 'a bluff'?" demanded the other.

Black shrugged his shoulders.

"I mean that there is no such organization as the 'Four Just Men.' They are a myth. They have no existence. It is too melodramatic for words. Imagine four people gathered together to correct the laws of England. It savours more of the sensational novel than of real life."

He laughed with apparent ease. "These things," he said, wagging his finger jocosely at the perturbed baronet, "do not happen in Pimlico. No, I suspect that our constable, the man I spoke to you about, is at the bottom of it. He is probably the whole Four of these desperate conspirators." He laughed again.

Sir Isaac fingered his moustache nervously. "It's all rot to say they don't exist; we know what they did six years ago, and I don't like this other man a bit," he grumbled.

"Don't like which other man?"

"This interfering policeman," he replied irritably. "Can't he be squared?"

"The constable?"

"Yes; you can square constables, I suppose, if you can square sergeants." Sir Isaac Tramber had the gift of heavy sarcasm.

Black stroked his chin thoughtfully.

"Curiously enough," he said, "I have never thought of that. I think we can try." He glanced at his watch. "Now I'll ask you just to clear out," he said. "I have an appointment at half-past one."

Sir Isaac smiled slowly.

"Rather a curious hour for an appointment," he said.

"Ours is a curious business," replied Colonel Black.

They rose, and Sir Isaac turned to Black.

"What is the appointment?" he asked.

Black smiled mysteriously.

"It is rather a peculiar case," he began.

He stopped suddenly.

There were hurried footsteps on the stairs without. A second later the door was flung open and Sparks burst into the room.

"Guv'nor," he gasped, "they're watching the house."

"Who is watching?"

"There's a busy* on the other side of the road," said the man, speaking graphically. "I spotted him, and the moment he saw I noticed him he moved off. He's back again now. Me and Willie have been watching him."

The two followed the agitated Sparks downstairs, where from a lower window they might watch, unobserved, the man who dared spy on their actions.

"If this is the police," fumed Black, "that dog Gurden has failed me. He told me Scotland Yard were taking no action whatever."

Frank, from his place of observation, was well aware that he had caused some consternation. He had seen Sparks turn back hurriedly with Jakobs and re-enter the house. He observed the light go out suddenly on the first floor, and now he had a pretty shrewd idea that they were watching him through the glass panel of the doorway.

There was no more he could learn. So far his business had been a failure. It was no secret to him that Sir Isaac Tramber was an associate of Black's, or that Jakobs and the estimable Sparks were also partners in this concern.

He did not know what he hoped to find, or what he had hoped to accomplish.

He was turning away in the direction of Victoria when his attention was riveted on the figure of a young man which was coming slowly along on the opposite sidewalk, glancing from time to time at the numbers which were inscribed on the fanlights of the doors.

* Busy: busy fellow, detective.

He watched him curiously, then in a flash he realized his objective as he stopped in front of No. 63.

In half a dozen steps he had crossed the road towards him. The boy – he was little more – turned round, a little frightened at the sudden appearance.

Frank Fellowe walked up to him and recognized him.

"You need not be scared," he said, "I am a police officer. Are you going into that house?"

The young man looked at him for a moment and made no reply. Then, in a voice that shook, he said "Yes."

"Are you going there to give Colonel Black certain information about your employer's business?"

The young man seemed hypnotized by fear.

He nodded.

"Is your employer aware of the fact?"

Slowly he shook his head.

"Did *he* send you?" he asked suddenly, and Frank observed a note of terror in his voice.

"No," he smiled, wondering internally who the "he" was. "I am here quite on my own, and my object is to warn you against trusting Colonel Black."

He jerked up his head and Frank saw the flush that came to his face.

"You are Constable Fellowe," he said suddenly.

To say that Frank was a little staggered is to express the position mildly.

"Yes," he repeated, "I am Constable Fellowe."

Whilst he was talking the door of the house had opened. From the position in which he stood Frank could not see this. Black merged stealthily and came down the steps towards him.

The agent had no other desire than to discover the identity of the man who was shadowing him. He was near enough to hear what the young man said.

"Fellowe," he boomed, and came down the rest of the steps at a run. "So it's you, is it?" he snarled. "It's you interfering with my business again."

"Something like that," said Frank coolly.

He turned to the young man again.

"I tell you," he said in a tone of authority, "that if you go into this house, or have anything whatever to do with this man, you will regret it to the last day of your life."

"You shall pay for this," fumed Black. "I'll have your coat from your back, constable. I'll give you in charge. I'll – I'll – "

"You have an excellent opportunity," said Frank. His quick eye had detected the figure of a constable on the other side of the road, walking slowly towards them. "There's a policeman over there; call him now and give me in charge. There is no reason why you shouldn't – no reason why you should want to avoid publicity of the act."

"Oh, no, no!"

It was the youth who spoke.

"Colonel Black, I must come another time."

He turned furiously on Frank.

"As to you" he began, gaining courage from Black's presence.

"As to you," retorted Frank, "avoid bad company!"

He hesitated, then turned and walked quickly away, leaving the two men alone on the pavement.

The three watchers in the hall eyed the scene curiously, and two of them at least anticipated instructions from Black which would not be followed by pleasant results for Frank.

With an effort, however, Black controlled his temper. He, too, had seen the shadow on the other side of the road.

"Look here, Constable Fellowe," he said, with forced geniality, "I know you're wrong, and you think you're right. Just come inside and let's argue this matter out."

He waited, his nimble mind evolving a plan for dealing with this dangerous enemy. He did not imagine that Frank would accept the invitation, and he was genuinely astounded when, without another word, the constable turned and slowly ascended the steps to the door.

39

THE MEN WHO SAT IN JUDGEMENT

Frank heard a little scuffling in the hall, and knew that the men who had been watching him had gone to cover. He had little fear, though he carried no weapon. He was supremely confident in his own strength and science.

Black, following him in, shut the door behind him. Frank heard the snick of a bolt being shot into its socket in the dark. Black switched on the light.

"We're playing fair, Constable Fellowe," he said, with an amiable smile. "You see, we do not try any monkey tricks with you. Everything is straight and above-board."

He led the way up the thickly-carpeted stairs, and Frank followed.

The young man noticed the house was luxuriously furnished. Rich engravings hung on the walls, the curtains that veiled the big stairway window were of silk, cabinets of Chinese porcelain filled the recesses.

Black led the way to a room on the first floor. It was not the room in which the board meeting had been held, but a small one which led off from the board-room.

Here the luxury was less apparent. Two desks formed the sole furniture of the room; the carpet under foot was of the commonplace type to be found in the average office. A great panel of tapestry – the one touch of luxury – covered one wall, and a cluster of lights in the ceiling afforded light to the room.

A little fire was burning in the grate. On a small table near one of the desks supper had been laid for two. Frank noticed this, and Black, inwardly cursing his own stupidity, smiled.

"It looks as though I expected you," he said easily, "though, as a matter of fact, I have some friends here tonight, and one of them is staying to supper."

Frank nodded. He knew the significance of that supper-table and the white paper pads ready for use.

"Sit down," said Black, and himself sat at one of the desks. Frank seated himself slowly at some distance from the other, half turning to face the man whom he had set himself to ruin.

"Now, let us get to business," said Black briskly. "There is no reason in the world why you and I should not have an understanding. I'm a business man, you're a business man, and a smart young man too," he said approvingly.

Frank made no reply. He knew what was coming.

"Now suppose," Black continued reflectively, "suppose we make an arrangement like this. You imagine that I am engaged in a most obnoxious type of business. Oh, I know!" he went on deprecatingly, "I know! You're under the impression that I'm making huge profits, that I'm robbing people by bucket-shop methods. I needn't tell you, constable, that I am most grieved and indignant that you should have entertained so low an opinion of my character."

His voice was neither grieved nor indignant. Indeed, the tone he employed was a cheerful admission of fault.

"Now, I am quite content you should investigate my affairs first hand. You know we receive a large number of accounts from all over the Continent and that we pay away enormous sums to clients who – well, shall we say – gamble on margins?"

"You can say what you like," said Frank. "Now," said Black, "suppose you go to Paris, constable, you can easily get leave, or go into the provinces, to any of the big towns in Great Britain where our clients reside, and interview them for yourself as to our honesty. Question them – I'll give you a list of them.

"I don't want you to do this at your own expense" – his big hands were outstretched in protest. "I don't suppose you have plenty of money to waste on that variety of excursion.

"Now, I will hand you tonight, if you like, a couple of hundred pounds, and you shall use this just as you like to further your investigations. How does that strike you?"

Frank smiled.

"It strikes me as devilish ingenious," he said. "I take the couple of hundred, and I can either use it for the purpose you mention or I can put it to my own account, and no questions will be asked. Do I understand aright?"

Colonel Black smiled and nodded. His strong, yellow face puckered in internal amusement.

"You are a singularly sharp young man," he said.

Frank rose.

"There's nothing doing," he said.

Colonel Black frowned.

"You mean you refuse?" he said.

Frank nodded.

"I refuse," he said, "absolutely. You can't bribe me with two hundred pounds, or with two thousand pounds, Black. I am not to be bought. I believe you are one of the most dangerous people society knows. I believe that both here and in the City you are running on crooked lines; I shall not rest until I have you in prison."

Black rose slowly to his feet.

"So that's it, is it?" he said.

There was menace and malignity in his tones. A look of implacable hatred met Fellowe's steady gaze.

"You will regret this," he went on gratingly. "I have given you a chance that most young men would jump at. I could make that three hundred – "

"If you were to make it thirty-three hundred, or thirty-three thousand," said Frank impatiently, "there would be no business done. I know you too well, Black. I know more about you than you think I know."

He took up his hat and examined the interior thoughtfully.

"There is a man wanted in France – an ingenious man who initiated Get-rich-quick banks all over the country, particularly in

Lyons and the South – his name is Olloroff," he said carefully. "There's quite a big reward offered for him. He had a partner who died suddenly – "

Black's face went white. The hand that rose to his lips shook a little.

"You know too much, I think," he said.

He turned swiftly and left the room. Frank sprang back to the door. He suspected treachery, but before he could reach it the door closed with a click.

He turned the handle and pulled, but it was fast.

He looked round the room, and saw another door at the farther end. He was half-way towards this when all the lights in the room went out. He was in complete darkness.

What he had thought to be a window at one end turned out to be a blank wall, so cunningly draped with curtains and ingeniously-shaped blinds as to delude the observer.

The real window, which looked out on to the street below, was heavily shuttered.

The absence of light was no inconvenience to him. He had a small electric lamp in his pocket, which he flashed round the room. It had been a tactical error on his part to put Black on his guard, but the temptation to give the big man a fright had been too great.

He realized that he was in a position of considerable danger. Save the young man he had seen in the street, and who in such an extraordinary manner had recognized him, nobody knew of his presence in that house.

He made a swift search of the room and listened intently at both doors, but he could hear nothing.

On the landing outside the door through which he had entered there were a number of antique Eastern arms hung on the wall. He had a slight hope that this scheme of decoration might have been continued in the room, but before he began his search he knew his quest was hopeless.

There would be no weapons here. He made a careful examination of the floor; he wanted to be on his guard against traps and pitfalls.

There was no danger from this. He sat down on the edge of a desk and waited.

He waited half an hour before the enemy gave a sign.

Then, close to his ear, it seemed, a voice asked: "Are you going to be sensible, constable?" Frank flashed the rays of his lamp in the direction from which the voice came.

He saw what appeared to him to be a hanging Eastern lantern. He had already observed that the stem from which it hung was unusually thick; now he realized that the bell-shaped lamp was the end of a speaking-tube.

He guessed, and probably correctly, that the device had been hung rather to allow Black to overhear than for the purpose of communicating with the occupants of the room.

He made no reply. Again the question was repeated, and he raised his head and answered.

"Come and see," he challenged.

All the time he had been waiting in the darkness his attention had been divided between the two doors. He was on the alert for the thin pencil of light which would show him the stealthy opening.

In some extraordinary manner he omitted to take into consideration the possibility of the outside lights being extinguished.

He was walking up and down the carpeted centre of the room, which was free of any impediment, when a slight noise behind him arrested his attention.

He had half turned when a noose was slipped over his body, a pair of desperate arms encircled his legs, and he was thrown violently to the floor.

He struggled, but it was against uneven odds. The lasso which had pinioned him prevented the free use of his arms. He found himself lying face downwards upon the carpet.

A handkerchief was thrust into his mouth, something cold and hard encircled his wrists and pulled them together. He heard a click, and knew that he was handcuffed behind.

"Pull him up," said Black's voice.

At that moment the lights in the room went on. Frank staggered to his feet, assisted urgently by Jakobs.

Black was there, Sparks was there, and a stranger Frank had seen enter the house was also there, but a silk handkerchief was fastened over the lower half of his face, and all that Frank could see was the upper half of a florid countenance and a pair of light blue eyes that twinkled shiftily.

"Put him on that sofa," said Black. "Now," he said, when his prisoner had been placed according to instructions, "I think you are going to listen to reason."

It was impossible for Frank Fellowe to reply. The handkerchief in his mouth was an effective bar to any retort that might have risen in his mind, but his eyes, clear, unwavering, spoke in unmistakable language to the smiling man who faced him.

"My proposition is very simple," said Black: "you're to hold your tongue, mind your own business, accept a couple of hundred on account, and you will not be further molested. Refuse, and I'm going to put you where I can think about you."

He smiled crookedly.

"There are some five cellars in this house," said Black; "if you are a student of history, as I am, Mr Fellowe, you should read the History of the Rhine Barons. You would recognize then that I have an excellent substitute for the donjon keeps of old. You will be chained there by the legs, you will be fed according to the whims of a trusted custodian, who, I may tell you, is a very absent-minded man, and there you will remain until you are either mad or glad – glad to accept our terms – or mad enough to be incarcerated in some convenient asylum, where nobody will take your accusations very seriously."

Black turned his head.

"Take that gag out," he said; "we will bring him into the other room. I do not think that his voice will be heard, however loudly he shouts, in there."

Jakobs pulled the handkerchief roughly from Frank's mouth. He was half pushed, half led, to the door of the board-room, which was in darkness.

Black went ahead and fumbled for the switch, the others standing in the doorway.

He found the light at last, and then he stepped back with a cry of horror.

Well he might, for four strangers sat at the board – four masked men.

The door leading into the board-room was a wide one. The three men with their prisoner stood grouped in the centre, petrified into immobility.

The four who sat at the table uttered no sound.

Black was the first to recover his self-possession. He started forward, then stopped. His face worked, his mouth opened, but he could frame no words.

"What – what?" he gasped.

The masked man who sat at the head of the table turned his bright eyes upon the proprietor of the establishment.

"You did not expect me, Mr Olloroff?" he said bluntly.

"My name is Black," said the other violently. "What are you doing here?"

"That you shall discover," said the masked man. "There are seats."

Then Black saw that seats had been arranged at the farther end of the table.

"First of all," the masked man went on, "I will relieve you of your prisoner. You take those handcuffs off, Sparks."

The man fumbled in his pocket for the key, but not in his waistcoat pocket – his hand went farther down.

"Keep your hand up," said the man at the table, sharply.

He made a little gesture with his hand, and Black's servant saw the gleam of a pistol.

"You need have no fear," he went on, "our little business will have no tragic sequence tonight – tonight!" he repeated significantly. "You have had three warnings from us, and we have come to deliver the last in person."

Black was fast recovering his presence of mind.

"Why not report to the police?" he scoffed.

"That we shall do in good time," was the polite reply, "but I warn you personally, Black, that you have almost reached the end of your tether."

In some ways Black was no coward. With an oath, he whipped out a revolver and sprang into the room.

As he did so the room went dark, and Frank found himself seized by a pair of strong hands and wrenched from the loose grip of his captor.

He was pushed forward, a door slammed behind him. He found himself tumbling down the carpeted stairs into the hall below. Quick hands removed the handcuffs from his wrists, the street door was opened by somebody who evidently knew the ways of the house, and he found himself, a little bewildered, in the open street, with two men in evening dress by his side.

They still wore their masks. There was nothing to distinguish either of them from the ordinary man in the street.

"This is your way, Mr Fellowe," said one, and he pointed up the street in the direction of Victoria.

Frank hesitated. He was keen to see the end of this adventure. Where were the other two of this vigilant four? Why had they been left behind? What were they doing?

His liberators must have guessed his thoughts, for one of them said, "Our friends are safe, do not trouble about them. You will oblige us, constable, by going very quickly."

With a word of thanks, Frank Fellowe turned and walked quickly up the street. He looked back once, but the two men had disappeared into the darkness.

THE EARL OF VERLOND

Colonel Black was amused. He was annoyed, too, and the two expressions resulted in a renewed irritation.

His present annoyance rose from another cause. A mysterious tribunal, which had examined his papers, had appeared from and disappeared to nowhere, had annoyed him – had frightened him, if the truth be told; but courage is largely a matter of light with certain temperaments, and strong in the security of the morning sunshine and with the satisfaction that there was nothing tangible for the four men to discover, he was bold enough.

He was sitting in his dressing-gown at breakfast, and his companion was Sir Isaac Tramber.

Colonel Black loved the good things of life, good food and the comforts of civilization. His breakfast was a very ample one.

Sir Isaac's diet was more simple: a brandy and water and an apple comprised the menu.

"What's up?" he growled. He had had a late night and was not in the best of tempers.

Black tossed a letter across to him.

"What do you think of that?" he asked. "Here's a demand from Tangye's, the brokers, for ten thousand pounds, and a hint that failing its arrival I shall be posted as a defaulter."

"Pay it," suggested Sir Isaac languidly, and the other laughed.

"Don't talk rot," he said, with offensive good humour. "Where am I going to get ten thousand pounds? I'm nearly broke; you know that, Tramber; we're both in the same boat. I've got two millions on paper, but I don't think we could raise a couple of hundred ready between us if we tried."

The baronet pushed back his plate.

"I say," he said abruptly, "you don't mean what you said?"

"About the money?

"About the money – yes. You nearly gave me an attack of heart disease. My dear chap, we should be pretty awkwardly fixed if money dried up just now."

Colonel Black smiled.

"That's just what has happened," he said. "Fix or no fix, we're in it. I'm overdrawn in the bank; I've got about a hundred pounds in the house, and I suppose you've got another hundred."

"I haven't a hundred farthings," said the other.

"Expenses are very heavy," Black went on; "you know how these things turn up. There are one or two in view, but beyond that we have nothing. If we could bring about the amalgamation of those Northern Foundries we might both sign cheques for a hundred thousand."

"What about the City?"

The Colonel sliced off the top of his egg without replying. Tramber knew the position in the City as well as he did.

"H'm," said Sir Isaac, "we've got to get money from somewhere, Black."

"What about your friend?" asked Colonel Black.

He spoke carelessly, but the question was a well-considered one.

"Which friend?" asked Sir Isaac, with a hoarse laugh. "Not that I have so many that you need particularize any. Do you mean Verlond?"

Black nodded.

"Verlond, my dear chap," said the baronet, "is the one man I must not go to in this world for money."

"He is a very rich man," mused Black.

"He is a very rich man," said the other grimly, "and he may have to leave his money to me."

"Isn't there an heir?" asked the colonel, interested.

"There was," said the baronet with a grin, "a high-spirited nephew, who ran away from home, and is believed to have been killed on a cattle-ranch in Texas. At any rate, Lord Verlond intends applying to the court to presume his death."

"That was a blow for the old man," said Black.

This statement seemed to amuse Sir Isaac. He leant back in his chair and laughed loud and long.

"A blow!" he said. "My dear fellow, he hated the boy worse than poison. You see, the Verlond stock – he's a member of the cadet branch of the family. The boy was a real Verlond. That's why the old man hated him. I believe he made his life a little hell. He used to have him up for weekends to bully him, until at last the kid got desperate, collected all his pocket-money and ran away.

"Some friends of the family traced him; the old man didn't move a step to search for him. They found work for him for a few months in a printer's shop in London. Then he went abroad – sailed to America on an emigrant's ticket.

"Some interested people took the trouble to follow his movements. He went out to Texas and got on to a pretty bad ranch. Later, a man after his description was shot in a street fight; it was one of those little ranching towns that you see so graphically portrayed in cinema palaces."

"Who is the heir?" asked Black.

"To the title, nobody. To the money, the boy's sister. She is quite a nice girl."

Black was looking at him through half-closed eyes.

The baronet curled his moustache thoughtfully and repeated, as if to himself, "Quite a nice girl."

"Then you have – er – prospects?" asked Black slowly.

"What the devil do you mean, Black?" asked Sir Isaac, sitting up stiffly.

"Just what I say," said the other. "The man who marries the lady gets a pretty large share of the swag. That's the position, isn't it?"

"Something like that," said Sir Isaac sullenly.

The colonel got up and folded his napkin carefully.

Colonel Black needed ready money so badly that it mattered very little what the City said. If Sandford objected that would be another matter, but Sandford was a good sportsman, though somewhat difficult to manage.

He stood for a moment looking down on the baronet thoughtfully.

"Ikey," he said, "I have noticed in you of late a disposition to look upon our mutual interests as something of which a man might be ashamed – I have struck an unexpected streak of virtue in you, and I confess that I am a little distressed."

His keen eyes were fixed on the other steadily.

"Oh, it's nothing," said the baronet uneasily, "but the fact is, I've got to keep my end up in society."

"You owe me a little," began Black.

"Four thousand," said the other promptly, "and it is secured by a £50,000 policy on my life."

"The premiums of which I pay," snarled the colonel grimly; "but I wasn't thinking of money."

His absorbed gaze took in the baronet from head to foot.

"Fifty thousand pounds!" he said facetiously. "My dear Ikey, you're worth much more murdered than alive."

The baronet shivered.

"Don't make those rotten jokes," he said, and finished his brandy at a gulp.

The other nodded.

"I'll leave you to your letters," he said.

Colonel Black was a remarkably methodical and neat personage. Wrapped in his elaborate dressing-gown, he made his way through the flat and, reaching his study alone, he closed the door behind him and let it click.

He was disturbed in his mind at this sudden assumption of virtue on the part of his confederate; it was more than disconcerting, it was alarming. Black had no illusions. He did not trust Sir Isaac Tramber any more than he did other men.

It was Black's money that had, to some extent, rehabilitated the baronet in society; it was Black's money that had purchased racehorses and paid training bills.

Here again, the man was actuated by no altruistic desire to serve one against whom the doors of society were shut and the hands of decent men were turned.

An outcast, Sir Isaac Tramber was of no value to the colonel: he had even, on one occasion, summarized his relationship with the baronet in a memorable and epigrammatic sentence: "He was the most dilapidated property I have ever handled; but I refurnished him, re-decorated him, and today, even if he is not beautiful, he is very letable."

And very serviceable Sir Isaac had proved – well worth the money spent on him, well worth the share he received from the proceeds of that business he professed to despise.

Sir Isaac Tramber feared Black. That was half the secret of the power which the stronger man wielded over him. When at times he sought to escape from the tyranny his partner had established, there were sleepless nights. During the past few weeks something had happened which made it imperative that he should dissociate himself from the confederacy; that "something" had to do with the brightening of his prospects.

Lady Mary Cassilirs was more of a reality now than she had ever been. With Lady Mary went that which Black in his vulgar way described as "swag."

The old earl had given him to understand that his addresses would not be unwelcome. Lady Mary was his ward, and perhaps it was because she refused to be terrorized by the wayward old man and his fits of savage moroseness, and because she treated his terrible storms of anger as though they did not exist and never had existed, that in the grim old man's hard and apparently wicked heart there had kindled a flame of respect for her.

Sir Isaac went back to his own chambers in a thoughtful frame of mind. He would have to cut Black, and his conscience had advanced so few demands on his actions that he felt justified in making an exception in this case.

He felt almost virtuous as he emerged again, dressed for the park, and he was in his brightest mood when he met Lord Verlond and his beautiful ward.

There were rude people who never referred to the Earl of Verlond and his niece except as "Beauty and the Beast."

She was a tall girl and typically English – straight of back, clear of skin, and bright of eye. A great mass of chestnut hair, two arched eyebrows, and a resolute little chin made up a face of special attractiveness.

She stood almost head and shoulders above the old man at her side. Verlond had never been a beauty. Age had made his harsh lines still harsher; there was not a line in his face which did not seem as though it had been carved from solid granite, so fixed, so immovable and cold it was.

His lower jaw protruded, his eyes were deep set. He gave you the uncanny impression when you first met him that you had been longer acquainted with his jaw than with his eyes.

He snapped a greeting to Sir Isaac.

"Sit down, Ikey," he smiled.

The girl had given the baronet the slightest of nods, and immediately turned her attention to the passing throng.

"Not riding today?" asked Sir Isaac.

"Yes," said the peer, "I am at this moment mounted on a grey charger, leading a brigade of cavalry."

His humour took this one form, and supplied answers to unnecessary questions.

Then suddenly his face went sour, and after a glance round to see whether the girl's attention had been attracted elsewhere, he leant over towards Sir Isaac and, dropping his voice, said, "Ikey, you're going to have some difficulty with her."

"I am used to difficulties," said Sir Isaac airily.

"Not difficulties like this," said the earl. "Don't be a fool, Ikey, don't pretend you're clever. I know – the difficulties – I have to live in the same house with her. She's an obstinate devil – there's no other word for it."

Sir Isaac looked round cautiously.

"Is there anybody else?" he asked.

He saw the earl's brows tighten, his eyes were glaring past him, and, following their direction, Sir Isaac saw the figure of a young man coming towards them with a smile that illuminated the whole of his face.

That smile was directed neither to the earl nor to his companion; it was unmistakably intended for the girl, who, with parted lips and a new light in her eyes, beckoned the newcomer forward.

Sir Isaac scowled horribly.

"The accursed cheek of the fellow," he muttered angrily.

"Good morning," said Horace Gresham to the earl; "taking the air?"

"No," growled the old man, "I am bathing, I am deep-sea fishing, I am aeroplaning. Can't you see what I am doing? I'm sitting here – at the mercy of every jackass that comes along to address his insane questions to me."

Horace laughed. He was genuinely amused. There was just this touch of perverse humour in the old man which saved him from being absolutely repulsive.

Without further ceremony he turned to the girl.

"I expected to find you here," he said.

"How is that great horse of yours?" she asked.

He shot a smiling glance at Tramber.

"Oh, he'll be fit enough on the day of the race," he said. "We shall make Timbolino gallop."

"Mine will beat yours, wherever they finish, for a thousand," said Sir Isaac angrily.

"I should not like to take your money," said the young man. "I feel that it would be unfair to you, and unfair to – your friend."

The last words said carelessly, but Sir Isaac Tramber recognized the undertone of hostility, and read in the little pause which preceded them the suggestion that this cheery young man knew much more about his affairs than he was prepared for the moment to divulge.

"I am not concerned about my friend," said the baronet angrily. "I merely made a fair and square sporting offer. Of course, if you do not like to accept it – " He shrugged his shoulders.

"Oh, I would accept it all right," said the other.

He turned deliberately to the girl.

"What's Gresham getting at?" asked Verlond, with a grin at his friend's discomfiture.

"I didn't know he was a friend of yours," said Sir Isaac; "where did you pick him up?"

Lord Verlond showed his yellow teeth in a grin.

"Where one picks up most of one's undesirable acquaintances," he said, "in the members' enclosure. But racing is getting so damned respectable, Ikey, that a real topnotch undesirable is hard to meet.

"The last race-meeting I went to, what do you think I found? The tea-room crammed, you couldn't get in at the doors; the bar empty. Racing is going to the dogs, Ikey."

He was on his favourite hobby now, and Sir Isaac shifted uneasily, for the old man was difficult to divert when in the mood for reminiscent chatter.

"You can't bet nowadays like you used to bet," the earl went on. "I once backed a horse for five thousand pounds at 20-1, without altering the price. Where could you do that nowadays?"

"Let us walk about a little," said the girl. Lord Verlond was so engrossed in his grievance against racing society that he did not observe the two young people rise and stroll away.

Sir Isaac saw them, and would have interrupted the other's garrulity, but for the wholesome fear he had of the old man's savage temper.

"I can't understand," said Horace, "how your uncle can stick that bounder."

The girl smiled.

"Oh, he can 'stick' him all right," she said dryly. "Uncle's patience with unpleasant people is proverbial."

"He's not very patient with me," said Mr Horace Gresham.

She laughed.

"That is because you are not sufficiently unpleasant," she said. "You have to be hateful to everybody else in the world before uncle likes you."

"And I'm not that, am I?" he asked eagerly.

She flushed a little.

"No, I wouldn't say you were that," she said, glancing at him from under her eyelashes. "I am sure you are a very nice and amiable young man. You must have lots of friends. Ikey, on the other hand, has such queer friends. We saw him at the Blitz the other day, lunching with a perfectly impossible man – do you know him?" she asked.

He shook his head.

"I don't know any perfectly impossible persons," he said promptly.

"A Colonel Black?" she suggested. He nodded.

"I know of him," he replied.

"Who is this Black?" she asked. "He is a colonel."

"In the army?

"Not in our army," said Horace with a smile. "He is what they call in America a 'pipe colonel,' and he's – well, he's a friend of Sir Isaac" he began, and hesitated.

"That doesn't tell me very much, except that he can't be very nice," she said.

He looked at her eagerly.

"I'm so glad you said that," he said. "I was afraid – " Again he stopped, and she threw a swift glance at him.

"You were afraid?" she repeated.

It was remarkable to see this self-possessed young man embarrassed, as he was now.

"Well," he went on, a little incoherently, "one hears things – rumours. I know what a scoundrel he is, and I know how sweet you are – the fact is, Mary, I love you better than anything in life."

She went white and her hand trembled. She had never anticipated such a declaration in a crowd. The unexpectedness of it left her speechless. She looked at his face: he, too, was pale.

"You shouldn't," she murmured, "at this time in the morning."

THE POLICEMAN AND A LADY

Frank Fellowe was agitating a punchball in one of the upper rooms of his little cottage, and with good reason.

He was "taking out" of the ball all the grievances he had against the petty irritants of life.

Sergeant Gurden had bothered him with a dozen and one forms of petty annoyance. He had been given the least congenial of jobs; he had been put upon melancholy point work; and he seemed to be getting more than his share of extra duty. And, in addition, he had the extra worry of checking, at the same time, the work of Black's organization. He might, had he wished, put away all the restrictions which hampered his movements, but that was not his way. The frustration of Black's plans was one of Frank's absorbing passions. If he had other passions which threatened to be equally absorbing, he had the sense to check them – for a while.

The daughter of a millionaire, violently introduced, subsequently met with heart-flutterings on the one side and not a little pertur-bation on the other; her gratitude and admiration began on a wayward two-seater with defective brakes, and progressed by way of the Zoo, for which she sent him a Sunday ticket – for she was anxious to see just what he was like.

She went in some fear of disillusionment, because an heroic constable in uniform, whose face is neatly arranged by helmet-peak and chin-strap, may be less heroic in clothes of his own choosing, to say nothing of cravats and shoes.

But she braced herself for the humiliation of discovering that one who could save her life could also wear a ready-made tie. She was terribly self-conscious, kept to the unfrequented walks of the Zoo, and was found by a very good-looking gentleman who was dressed irreproachably in something that suggested neither the butcher's boy at a beanfeast nor a plumber at a funeral.

She showed him the inmates of exactly two cages, then he took her in hand and told her things about wild beasts that she had never known before. He showed her the subtle distinction between five varieties of lynx, and gave her little anecdotes of the jungle fellowship that left her breathless with admiration. Moreover, he took her to the most unlikely places – to rooms where the sick and lame of the animal kingdom were nursed to health. It would appear that there was no need to have sent him the ticket, because he was a Fellow of the Society.

There was too much to be seen on one day. She went again and yet again; rode with him over Hampstead Heath in the early hours of the morning. She gathered that he jobbed his horse, yet it was not always the same animal he rode.

"How many horses have you in your stable?" she asked banteringly one morning.

"Six," he said readily. "You see," he added hastily, "I do a lot of hunting in the season – "

He stopped, realizing that he was further in the mire.

"But you are a constable – a policeman!" she stammered. "I mean – forgive me if I'm rude."

He turned in his saddle, and there was a twinkle in his eye.

"I have a little money of my own," he said. "You see, I have only been a constable for twelve months; previous to that I – I wasn't a constable!"

He was not very lucid: by this time he was apparently embarrassed, and she changed the subject, wondering and absurdly pleased.

It was inconsistent of her to realize after the ride that these meetings were wrong. They were wrong before, surely? Was it worse to ride with a man who had revealed himself to be a member of one's own class than with a policeman? Nevertheless, she knew it was wrong and met him – and that is where Constable Fellowe and Miss Sandford became "May" and "Frank" to one another. There had been nothing clandestine in their meetings.

Theodore Sandford, a hard-headed man, was immensely democratic.

He joked about May's policeman, made ponderous references to stolen visits to his palatial kitchen in search of rabbit pie, and then there arose from a jesting nothing the question of Frank's remaining in the force. He had admitted that he had independent means. Why remain a ridiculous policeman?

From jest it had passed into a very serious discussion and the presentation of an ultimatum, furiously written, furiously posted, and as furiously regretted.

Theodore Sandford looked up from his writing-table with an amused smile.

"So you're really angry with your policeman, are you?" he asked.

But it was no joke to the girl. Her pretty face was set determinedly.

"Of course," she shrugged her pretty shoulders, "Mr Fellowe can do as he wishes – I have no authority over him" – this was not true – "but one is entitled to ask of one's friends – "

There were tears of mortification in her eyes, and Sandford dropped his banter. He looked at the girl searchingly, anxiously. Her mother had died when May was a child; he was ever on the look-out for some sign of the fell disease which carried off the woman who had been his all.

"Dearest!" he said tenderly "you mustn't be worried or bothered by your policeman; I'm sure he'd do anything in the world for you, if he is only half a human man. You aren't looking well," he said anxiously.

She smiled.

"I'm tired tonight, daddy," she said, putting her arm about his neck.

"You're always tired nowadays," he said. "Black thought so the other day when he saw you. He recommended a very clever doctor – I've got his address somewhere."

She shook her head with vigour.

"I don't want to see doctors," she said decidedly.

"But – "

"Please – please!" she pleaded, laughing now. "You mustn't!"

There was a knock at the door and a footman came in.

"Mr Fellowe, madam," he announced.

The girl looked round quickly.

"Where is he?" she asked.

Her father saw the pink in her cheeks and shook his head doubtingly.

"He is in the drawing-room," said the man.

"I'll go down, daddy." She turned to her father.

He nodded.

"I think you'll find he's fairly tractable – by the way, the man is a gentleman."

"A gentleman, daddy!" she answered with lofty scorn, "of course he's a gentleman!"

"I'm sorry I mentioned it," said Mr Theodore Sandford humbly.

Frank was reading her letter – the letter which had brought him to her – when she came in.

He took her hand and held it for a fraction of a second, then he came straight to the point.

It was hard enough, for never had she so appealed to him as she did this night.

There are some women whose charms are so elusive, whose beauty is so unordinary in character, as to baffle adequate description.

May Sandford was one of these.

No one feature goes to the making of a woman, unless, indeed, it be her mouth. There is something in the poise of the head, in the method of arranging the hair, in the clearness and peach-like bloom of the complexion, in the carriage of the shoulders, the suppleness of the body, the springy tread – each characteristic furnished something to the beautiful whole.

May Sandford was a beautiful girl. She had been a beautiful child, and had undergone none of the transition from prettiness to plainness, from beauty to awkwardness. It was as though the years had each contributed their quota to the creation of the perfect woman.

"Surely," he said, "you do not mean this? That is not your view?" He held out her letter.

She bent her head.

"I – I think it would be best," she said in a low tone. "I don't think we shall agree very well on – on things. You've been rather horrid lately, Mr Fellowe."

His face was very pale.

"I don't remember that I have been particularly horrid," he said quietly.

"It is impossible for you to remain a policeman," she went on tremulously. She went up to him and laid her hands upon his shoulders. "Don't you see – even papa jokes about it, and it's horrid. I'm sure the servants talk – and I'm not a snob really – "

Frank threw back his head and laughed.

"Can't you see, dearie, that I should not be a policeman if there was not excellent reason? I am doing this work because I have promised my superior that I would do it."

"But – but," she said, bewildered, "if you left the force you would have no superior."

"I cannot give up my work," he said simply.

He thought a moment, then shook his head slowly.

"You ask me to break my word," he said. "You ask me to do greater mischief than that which I am going to undo. You wouldn't you couldn't, impose that demand upon me.'

She drew back a little, her head raised, pouting ever so slightly.

"I see," she said, "you would not." She held out her hand. "I shall never ask you to make another sacrifice."

He took her hand, held it tightly a moment, then let it drop. Without another word the girl left the room. Frank waited a moment, hoping against hope that she would repent. The door remained closed.

He left the house with an overwhelming sense of depression.

DR ESSLEY MEETS A MAN

Dr Essley was in his study, making a very careful microscopic examination. The room was in darkness save for the light which came from a powerful electric lamp directed to the reflector of the instrument. What he found on the slide was evidently satisfactory, for by and by he removed the strip of glass, threw it into the fire and turned on the lights.

He took up a newspaper cutting from the table and read it.

It interested him, for it was an account of the sudden death of Mr Augustus Fanks.

"The deceased gentleman," ran the account, "was engaged with Colonel Black, the famous financier, discussing the details of the new iron amalgamation, when he suddenly collapsed and, before medical assistance could be procured, expired, it is believed, of heart failure."

There had been no inquest, for Fanks had in truth a weak heart and had been under the care of a specialist, who, since his speciality was heart trouble, discovered symptoms of the disease on the slightest pretext.

So that was the end of Fanks. The doctor nodded slowly. Yes, that was the end of him. And now?

He took a letter from his pocket. It was addressed to him in the round sprawling calligraphy of Theodore Sandford.

Essley had met him in the early days when Sandford was on friendly terms with Black. He had been recommended to the ironmaster by the financier, and had treated him for divers ills. "My suburban doctor," Sandford had called him.

"Though I am not seeing eye to eye with our friend Black," he wrote, "and we are for the moment at daggers drawn, I trust that this will not affect our relationships, the more so since I wish you to see my daughter."

Essley remembered having seen her once: a tall girl, with eyes that danced with laughter and a complexion of milk and roses.

He put the letter in his pocket, went into his little surgery and locked the door. When he came out he wore his long overcoat and carried a little satchel. He had just time to catch a train for the City, and at eleven o'clock he found himself in Sandford's mansion.

"You are a weird man, doctor," said the ironmaster with a smile, as he greeted his visitor. "Do you visit most of your patients by night?"

"My aristocratic patients," said the other coolly.

"A bad job about poor Fanks," said the other. "He and I were only dining together a few weeks ago. Did he tell you that he met a man who knew you in Australia?"

A shadow of annoyance passed over the other's face.

"Let us talk about your daughter," he said brusquely. "What is the matter with her?"

The ironmaster smiled sheepishly. "Nothing, I fear; yet you know, Essley, she is my only child, and I sometimes imagine that she is looking ill. My doctor in Newcastle tells me that there is nothing wrong with her."

"I see," said Essley. "Where is she?"

"She is at the theatre," confessed the father. "You must think I am an awful fool to bring you up to town to discuss the health of a girl who is at the theatre, but something upset her pretty badly last night, and I was today glad to see her take enough interest in life to visit a musical comedy."

"Most fathers are fools," said the other. "I will wait till she comes in." He strolled to the window and looked out.

"Why have you quarrelled with Black?" he asked suddenly.

The older man frowned.

"Business," he said shortly. "He is pushing me into a corner. I helped him four years ago — "

"He helped you, too," interrupted the doctor.

"But not so much as I helped him," said the other obstinately. "I gave him his chance. He floated my company and I profited, but he profited more. The business has now grown to such vast proportions that it will not pay me to come in. Nothing will alter my determination."

"I see." Essley whistled a little tune as he walked again to the window.

Such men as this must be broken, he thought. Broken! And there was only one way: that daughter of his. He could do nothing tonight, that was evident – nothing.

"I do not think I will wait for your daughter," he said. "Perhaps I will call in tomorrow evening."

"I am so sorry – "

But the doctor silenced him.

"There is no need to be sorry," he said with acerbity; "you will find my visit charged in my bill."

The ironmaster laughed as he saw him to the door.

"You are almost as good a financier as your friend," he said.

"Almost," said the doctor dryly.

His waiting taxi dropped him at Charing Cross, and he went straight to the nearest call-office and rang up a Temperance Hotel at Bloomsbury.

He had reasons for wishing to meet a Mr Weld who knew him in Australia.

He had no difficulty in getting the message through. Mr Weld was in the hotel. He waited whilst the attendant found him. By and by a voice spoke: "I am Weld – do you want me?"

"Yes; my name is Cole. I knew you in Australia. I have a message for you from a mutual friend. Can you see me tonight?"

"Yes; where?"

Dr Essley had decided the place of meeting. "Outside the main entrance of the British Museum," he said. "There are few people about at this time of night, and I am less likely to miss you."

There was a pause at the other end of the wire.

"Very good," said the voice; "in a quarter of an hour?"

"That will suit me admirably – goodbye." He hung up the receiver. Leaving his satchel at the cloak-room at Charing Cross Station, he set out to walk to Great Russell Street. He would take no cab. There should be no evidence of that description. Black would not like it. He smiled at the thought. Great Russell Street was deserted, save for a constant stream of taxi-cabs passing and repassing and an occasional pedestrian. He found his man waiting; rather tall and slight, with an intellectual, refined face.

"Dr Essley?" he asked, coming forward as the other halted.

"That is my – "

Essley stopped.

"My name is Cole," he said harshly. "What made you think I was Essley?"

"Your voice," said the other calmly. "After all, it does not matter what you call yourself; I want to see you."

"And I you," said Essley.

They walked along side by side until they came to a side street.

"What do you want of me?" asked the doctor.

The other laughed.

"I wanted to see you. You are not a bit like the Essley I knew. He was slighter and had not your colouring, and I was always under the impression that the Essley who went up into the bush died."

"It is possible," said Essley in an absent way. He wanted to gain time. The street was empty. A little way down there was a gateway in which a man might lie unobserved until a policeman came.

In his pocket he had an impregnated feather carefully wrapped up in lint and oiled silk. He drew it from his pocket furtively and with his hands behind him he stripped it of its covering.

"...in fact, Dr Essley," the man was saying, "I am under the impression that you are an impostor."

Essley faced him.

"You think too much," he said in a low voice, "and after all, I do not recognize – turn your face to the light."

65

The young man obeyed. It was a moment. Quick as thought the doctor raised the feather…

A hand of steel gripped his wrist. As if from the ground, two other men had appeared. Something soft was thrust into his face; a sickly aroma overpowered him. He struggled madly, but the odds were too many, and then a shrill police-whistle sounded and he dropped to the ground…

He awoke to find a policeman bending over him. Instinctively he put his hand to his head.

"Hurt, sir?" asked the man.

"No."

He struggled to his feet and stood unsteadily.

"Did you capture the men?"

"No, sir, they got away. We just spotted them as they downed you, but, bless your heart, they seemed to be swallowed up by the earth."

He looked around for the feather: it had disappeared. With some reluctance he gave his name and address to the constable, who called a taxi-cab.

"You're sure you've lost nothing, sir?" asked the man.

"Nothing," said Essley testily. "Nothing – look here, constable, do not report this." He slipped a pound into the man's hand. "I do not wish this matter to get into the papers."

The constable handed the money back.

"I'm sorry, sir," he said, "I couldn't take this even if I was willing." He looked round quickly and lowered his voice. "I've got a gentleman from the Yard with me," he said, "one of the assistant commissioners."

Essley followed the direction of the policeman's eyes. In the shadow of the wall a man was standing.

"He was the chap who saw you first," said the policeman, young and criminally loquacious.

Obeying some impulse he could not define, Essley walked towards the man in the shadow.

"I owe you a debt of gratitude," he said. "I can only hope that you will add to your kindness by letting the matter drop – I should hate to see the thing referred to in the newspapers."

"I suppose you would," said the unknown. He was in evening dress, and the red glow of his cigar rather concealed than defined his face. "But this is a matter, Dr Essley, where you must allow us full discretion."

"How do you know my name?" asked the doctor suspiciously.

The other smiled in the darkness and turned away.

"One moment!"

Essley took a stride forward and peered into the other's face.

"I seem to recognize your voice," he said.

"That is possible" said the other, and pushed him gently, but firmly, away.

Essley gasped. He himself was no weakling, but this man had an arm like steel.

"I think you had better go, sir," said the police constable anxiously. He desired neither to offend an obviously influential member of the public nor his superior – that mysterious commissioner who appeared and disappeared in the various divisions and who left behind him innumerable casualties amongst the different members of the force.

"I'll go," said the doctor, "but I should like to know this gentleman's name."

"That cannot possibly interest you," said the stranger, and Essley shrugged his shoulders.

With that he had to be content. He drove home to Forest Hill, thinking, thinking.

Who were these three – what object had they?

Who was the man who had stood in the shadows? Was it possible that his assailants were acting in collusion with the police?

He was no nearer the solution when he reached his home. He unlocked the door and let himself in. There was nobody in the house but himself and the old woman upstairs.

His comings and goings were so erratic that he had organized a system which allowed him the most perfect freedom of movement.

There must be an end to Dr Essley, he decided. Essley must disappear from London. He need not warn Black – Black would know.

He would settle the business of the iron-master and his daughter, and then – there would be a finish.

He unlocked his study, entered and switched on the lights.

There was a letter on his writing-table, a letter enclosed in a thin grey envelope. He picked it up and examined it. It had been delivered by hand, and bore his name written in a firm hand.

He looked at the writing-table and started back.

The letter had been written in the room and blotted on the pad!

There was no doubt at all about it. The blotting-paper had been placed there fresh that day, and the reverse of the bold handwriting on the envelope was plain to see.

He looked at the envelope again.

It could not have been a patient: he never admitted patients – he had none worth mentioning. The practice was a blind. Besides, the door had been locked, and he alone had the key. He tore the envelope open and took out the contents. It was a half-sheet of notepaper. The three lines of writing ran –

You escaped tonight, and have only seven days to prepare yourself for the fate which awaits you.

'THE FOUR JUST MEN.'

He sank into his chair, crushed by the knowledge.

They were the Just Men – and he had escaped them.

The Just Men! He buried his face in his hands and tried to think. Seven days they gave him. Much could be done in seven days. The terror of death was upon him, he who had without qualm or remorse sent so many on the long journey. But this was he – himself! He clutched at his throat and glared round the room. Essley the poisoner – the expert; a specialist in death – the man who had revived the lost art of the Medicis and had hoodwinked the law. Seven days! Well, he would settle the business of the ironmaster. That was necessary to Black.

He began to make feverish preparations for the future. There were no papers to destroy. He went into the surgery and emptied three bottles down the sink. The fourth he would want. The fourth had been useful to Black: a little green bottle with a glass stopper. He slipped it into his pocket.

He let the tap run to wash away all trace of the drug he had spilt. The bottles he smashed and threw into a waste-bin.

He went upstairs to his room, but he could not sleep. He locked his door and put a chair against it. With a revolver in his hand, he searched the cupboard and beneath the bed. He placed the revolver under his pillow and tried to sleep.

Next morning found him haggard and ill, but none the less he made his toilet with customary care.

Punctually at noon he presented himself at Hampstead and was shown into the drawing-room.

The girl was alone when he entered. He noted with approval that she was very beautiful.

That May Sandford did not like him he knew by instinct. He saw the cloud come to her pretty face as he came into her presence, and was amused in his cold way.

"My father is out," she said.

"That is good," said Essley, "for now we can talk."

He seated himself without invitation.

"I think it is only right to tell you, Dr Essley, that my father's fears regarding me are quite groundless."

At that moment the ironmaster came in and shook hands warmly with the doctor.

"Well, how do you think she looks?" he asked.

"Looks tell you nothing," said the other. It was not the moment for the feather. He had other things to do, and the feather was not the way. He chatted for a while and then rose. "I will send you some medicine," he said.

She pulled a wry face.

"You need not worry to take it," he said, with the touch of rancour that was one of his characteristics.

"Can you come to dinner on Tuesday?" asked Sandford.

Essley considered. This was Saturday – three days out of seven, and anything might turn up in the meantime.

"Yes," he said, "I will come."

He took a cab to some chambers near the Thames Embankment. He had a most useful room there.

COLONEL BLACK HAS A SHOCK

Mr Sandford had an appointment with Colonel Black. It was the final interview before the break.

The City was busy with rumours. A whisper had circulated; all was not well with the financier – the amalgamation on which so much depended had not gone through.

Black sat at his desk that afternoon, idly twiddling a paper-knife. He was more sallow than usual; the hand that held the knife twitched nervously.

He looked at his watch. It was time Sandford came. He pushed a bell by the side of his desk and a clerk appeared.

"Has Mr Sandford arrived?" he asked.

"He has just come, sir," said the man.

"Show him in."

The two men exchanged formal greetings, and Black pointed to a chair.

"Sit down, Sandford," he said curtly. "Now, exactly how do we stand?"

"Where we did," said the other uncompromisingly.

"You will not come into my scheme?"

"I will not," said the other.

Colonel Black tapped the desk with his knife, and Sandford looked at him. He seemed older than when he had last seen him. His yellow face was seamed and lined.

"It means ruin for me," he said suddenly. "I have more creditors than I can count. If the amalgamation went through I should be

71

established. There are lots of people in with me too – Ikey Tramber –
you know Sir Isaac? He's a friend of – er – the Earl of Verlond."

But the elder man was not impressed.

"It is your fault if you're in a hole," said he. "You have taken on too
big a job – more than that, you have taken too much for granted."

The man at the desk looked up from under his straight brows.

"It is all very well for you to sit there and tell me what I should
do," he said, and the shakiness of his voice told the other something
of the passion he concealed. "I do not want advice or homily – I want
money. Come into my scheme and amalgamate, or – "

"Or – " repeated the ironmaster quietly.

"I do not threaten you," said Black sullenly; "I warn you. You are
risking more than you know."

"I'll take the risk," said Sandford. He got up on to his feet. "Have
you anything more to say?"

"Nothing."

"Then I'll bid you goodbye."

The door closed with a slam behind him, and Black did not move.
He sat there until it was dark, doing no more than scribble aimlessly
upon his blotting-pad.

It was nearly dark when he drove back to the flat he occupied in
Victoria Street and let himself in.

"There is a gentleman waiting to see you, sir," said the man who
came hurrying to help him out of his coat.

"What sort of a man?"

"I don't know exactly, sir, but I have got a feeling that he is a
detective."

"A detective?" He found his hands trembling, and cursed his folly.
He stood uncertainly in the centre of the hall. In a minute he had
mastered his fears and turned the handle of the door.

A man rose to meet him.

He had a feeling that he had met him before. It was one of those
impressions that it is so difficult to explain.

"You wanted to see me?" he asked.

"Yes, sir," said the man, a note of deference in his voice. "I have called to make a few inquiries."

It was on the tip of Black's tongue to ask him whether he was a police officer, but somehow he had not the courage to frame the words.

The effort was unnecessary, as it proved, for the next words of the man explained his errand.

"I have been engaged," he said, "by a firm of solicitors to discover the whereabouts of Dr Essley."

Black looked hard at him. "There ought to be no difficulty," he said, "in that. The doctor's name is in the Directory."

"That is so," said the man, "and yet I have had the greatest difficulty in running him to earth. As a matter of fact," explained the man, "I was wrong when I said I wanted to discover his whereabouts. It is his identity I wish to establish."

"I do not follow you," said the financier.

"Well," said the man, "I don't know exactly how to put it. If you know Dr Essley, you will recall the fact that he was for some years in Australia."

"That is true," said Black. "He and I came back together."

"And you were there some years, sir?"

"Yes, we were there for a number of years, though we were not together all the time."

"I see," said the man. "You went out together, I believe?

"No," replied the other sharply, "we went at different periods."

"Have you seen him recently?"

"No, I have not seen him, although I have frequently written to him on various matters." Black was trying hard not to lose his patience. It would not do for this man to see how much the questions were irritating him.

The man jotted down something in his notebook, closed it and put it in his pocket.

"Would you be surprised to learn," he asked quietly, "that the real Dr Essley who went out to Australia died there?"

Black's fingers caught the edge of the table and he steadied himself.

"I did not know that," he said. "Is that all you have to ask?" he said, as the man finished.

"I think that will do, sir," said the detective.

"Can I ask you on whose behalf you are inquiring?" demanded the colonel.

"That I am not at liberty to tell."

After he had gone, Black paced the apartment, deep in thought.

He took down from the shelf a continental Baedeker and worked out with a pencil and paper a line of retirement. The refusal of Sandford to negotiate with him was the crowning calamity.

He crossed the room to the safe which stood in the corner, and opened it. In the inside drawer were three flat packets of notes. He picked them out and laid them on the table. They were notes on the Bank of France, each for a thousand francs.

It would be well to take no risks. He put them in the inside pocket of his coat. If all things failed, they were the way to freedom.

As for Essley – he smiled. He must go any way.

He left his flat and drove eastwards to the City.

Two men followed him, though this he did not know.

Black boasted that his corporation kept no books, maintained no record, and this fact was emphasized the night that the Four had visited him unbidden. Their systematic search for evidence, which they had intended to use against him at a recognized tribunal, had failed to disclose the slightest vestige of documentary evidence which might be employed.

Yet, if the truth be told, Black kept a very complete set of books, only they were in a code of his own devising, the key of which he had never put on paper, and which he only could understand.

He was engaged on the evening of the detective's visit in placing even these ledgers beyond the reach of the Four. He had good reason for his uneasiness.

The Four had been very active of late, and they had thought fit to issue another challenge to Colonel Black.

He was busy from nine o'clock to eleven, tearing up apparently innocent letters and burning them. When that hour struck, he looked at his watch and confirmed the time. He had very important business that night.

He wrote a note to Sir Isaac Tramber, asking him to meet him that night. He had need of every friend, every pull, and every bit of help that could come to him.

LORD VERLOND GIVES A DINNER

Lord Verlond was an afternoon visitor at the Sandford establishment. He had come for many reasons, not the least of which nobody expected. He was a large shareholder in the Sandford Foundries, and with rumours of amalgamation in the air there was excuse enough for his visit. Doubly so, it seemed, when the first person he met was a large, yellow-faced man, confoundedly genial (in the worst sense of the word) and too ready to fraternize for the old man's liking.

"I have heard of you, my lord," said Colonel Black.

"For the love of Heaven, don't call me 'my lord'!" snapped the earl. "Man alive, you are asking me to be rude to you!"

But no man of Verlond's standing could be rude to the colonel, with his mechanical smile and his beaming eye.

"I know a friend of yours, I think," he said, in that soothing tone which in a certain type of mind passes for deference.

"You know Ikey Tramber, which is not the same thing," said the earl.

Colonel Black made a noise indicating his amusement.

"He always – " he began.

"He always speaks well of me and says what a fine fellow I am, and how the earth loses its savour if he passes a day without seeing me," assisted Lord Verlond, his eyes alight with pleasant malice, "and he tells you what a good sportsman I am, and what a true and kindly heart beats behind my somewhat unprepossessing exterior, and how if people only knew me they would love me – he says all this, doesn't he?"

Colonel Black bowed.

"I don't think!" said Lord Verlond vulgarly.

He looked at the other for a while.

"You shall come to dinner with me tonight – you will meet a lot of people who will dislike you intensely."

"I shall be delighted," murmured the colonel.

He was hoping that in the conference which he guessed would be held between Sandford and his lordship he would be invited to participate.

In this, however, he was disappointed. He might have taken his leave there and then, but he chose to stay and discuss art (which he imperfectly understood) with a young and distracted lady who was thinking about something else all the time.

She badly wanted to bring the conversation round to the Metropolitan police force, in the hope that a rising young constable might be mentioned. She would have asked after him, but her pride prevented her. Colonel Black himself did not broach the subject.

He was still discussing lost pictures when Lord Verlond emerged from the study with Sandford.

"Let your daughter come," the earl was saying.

Sandford was undecided.

"I'm greatly obliged – I should not like her to go alone."

Something leapt inside Colonel Black's bosom. A chance…!

"If you are talking of the dinner tonight," he said with an assumption of carelessness, "I shall be happy to call in my car for you."

Still Sandford was not easy in his mind. It was May who should make the decision.

"I think I'd like to, daddy," she said.

She did not greatly enjoy the prospect of going anywhere with the colonel, but it would only be a short journey.

"If I could stand *in loco parentis* to the young lady," said Black, nearly jocular, "I should esteem it an honour."

He looked round and caught a curious glint in Lord Verlond's eyes. The earl was watching him closely, eagerly, almost, and a sudden and unaccountable fear gripped the financier's heart.

"Excellent, excellent!" murmured the old man, still watching him through lowered lids. "It isn't far to go, and I think you'll stand the journey well."

The girl smiled, but the grim fixed look on the earl's face did not relax.

"As you are an invalid, young lady," he went on, despite May's laughing protest – "as you're an invalid, young lady, I will have Sir James Bower and Sir Thomas Bigland to meet you – you know those eminent physicians, colonel? Your Dr Essley will, at any rate – experts both on the action of vegetable alkaloids."

Great beads of sweat stood on Black's face, but his features were under perfect control. Fear and rage glowed in his eyes, but he met the other's gaze defiantly. He smiled even – a slow, laboured smile.

"That puts an end to any objection," he said almost gaily.

The old man took his leave and was grinning to himself all the way back to town.

The Earl of Verlond was a stickler for punctuality: a grim, bent old man, with a face that, so Society said, told eloquently the story of his life, his bitter tongue was sufficient to maintain for him the respect – or if not the respect, the fear that so ably substitutes respect – of his friends.

"Friends" is a word which you would never ordinarily apply to any of the earl's acquaintances. He had apparently no friends save Sir Isaac Tramber.

"I have people to dine with me," he had said cynically when this question of friendship was once discussed by one who knew him sufficiently well to deal with so intimate a subject.

That night he was waiting in the big library of Carnarvon Place. The earl was one of those men who observed a rigid time-table every day of his life.

He glanced at his watch; in two minutes he would be on his way to the drawing-room to receive his guests.

Horace Gresham was coming. A curious invitation, Sir Isaac Tramber had thought, and had ventured to remark as much, presuming his friendship.

78

"When I want your advice as to my invitation list, Ikey," said the earl, "I will send you a prepaid telegram."

"I thought you hated him," grumbled Sir Isaac.

"Hate him! Of course I hate him. I hate everybody. I should hate you, but you are such an insignificant devil," said the earl. "Have you made your peace with Mary?"

I don't know what you mean by 'making my peace,' " said Sir Isaac complainingly. "I tried to be amiable to her, and I only seemed to succeed in making a fool of myself."

"Ah!" said the nobleman with a little chuckle, "she would like you best natural."

Sir Isaac shot a scowling glance at his patron.

"I suppose you know," he said, "that I want to marry Mary."

"I know that you want some money without working for it," said the earl. "You have told me about it twice. I am not likely to forget it. It is the sort of thing I think about at nights."

"I wish you wouldn't pull my leg," growled the baronet. "Are you waiting for any other guests?

"No," snarled the earl, "I am sitting on the top of Mont Blanc eating rice pudding."

There was no retort to this.

"I've invited quite an old friend of yours," said the earl suddenly, "but it doesn't look as if he was turning up."

Ikey frowned.

"Old friend?"

The other nodded.

"Military gent," he said laconically. "A colonel in the army, though nobody knows the army."

Sir Isaac's jaw dropped.

"Not Black?"

Lord Verlond nodded. He nodded several times, like a gleeful child confessing a fault of which it was inordinately proud.

"Black it is," he said, but made no mention of the girl.

He looked at his watch again and pulled a little face.

"Stay here," he commanded. "I'm going to telephone."

"Can I –"

"You can't!" snapped the earl.

He was gone some time, and when he returned to the library there was a smile on his face.

"Your pal's not coming," he said, and offered no explanation either for the inexplicable behaviour of the colonel or for his amusement.

At dinner Horace Gresham found himself seated next to the most lovely woman in the world. She was also the kindest and the easiest to amuse. He was content to forget the world, and such of the world who were gathered about the earl, but Lord Verlond had other views.

"Met a friend of yours today," he said abruptly and addressing Horace.

"Indeed, sir?" The young man was politely interested.

"Sandford – that terribly prosperous gentleman from Newcastle."

Horace nodded cautiously.

"Friend of yours too, ain't he?" The old man turned swiftly to Sir Isaac. "I asked his daughter to come to dinner – father couldn't come. She ain't here."

He glared round the table for the absent girl.

"In a sense Sandford is a friend of mine," said Sir Isaac no less cautiously, since he must make a statement in public without exactly knowing how the elder man felt on the subject of the absent guests; "at least, he's a friend of a friend."

"Black," snarled Lord Verlond, "bucket shop swindler – are you in it?"

"I have practically severed my connection with him," Sir Isaac hastened to say.

Verlond grinned.

"That means he's broke," he said, and turned to Horace. "Sandford's full of praise for a policeman who's mad keen on his girl – friend of yours?"

Horace nodded.

"He's a great friend of mine," he said quietly.

"Who is he?"

"Oh, he's a policeman," said Horace. "And I suppose he's got two legs and a head and a pair of arms," said the earl. "You're too full of information – I know he's a policeman. Everybody seems to be talking about him. Now, what does he do, where does he come from – what the devil does it all mean?"

"I'm afraid I can't give you any information," said Horace. "The only thing that I am absolutely certain about in my own mind is that he is a gentleman."

"A gentleman and a policeman?" asked the earl incredulously.

Horace nodded.

"A new profession for the younger son, eh?" remarked Lord Verlond sardonically. "No more running away and joining the army; no more serving before the mast; no more cow-punching on the pampas – "

A look of pain came into Lady Mary's eyes. The old lord swung round on her.

"Sorry," he growled. "I wasn't thinking of that young fool. No more dashing away to the ends of the earth for the younger son; no dying picturesquely in the Cape Mounted Rifles, or turning up at an appropriate hour with a bag of bullion under each arm to save the family from ruin. Join the police force, that's the game. You ought to write a novel about that: a man who can write letters to the sporting papers can write anything."

"By the way," he added, "I am coming down to Lincoln on Tuesday to see that horse of yours lose."

"You will make your journey in vain," said Horace. "I have arranged for him to win."

He waited later for an opportunity to say a word in private to the old man. It did not come till the end of the dinner, when he found himself alone with the earl.

"By the way," he said, with an assumption of carelessness, "I want to see you on urgent private business."

"Want money?" asked the earl, looking at him suspiciously from underneath his shaggy brows.

Horace smiled.

"No, I don't think I am likely to borrow money," he said.

"Want to marry my niece?" asked the old man with brutal directness.

"That's it," said Horace coolly. He could adapt himself to the old man's mood.

"Well, you can't," said the earl. "You have arranged for your horse to win, I have arranged for her to marry Ikey. At least," he corrected himself, "Ikey has arranged with me."

"Suppose she doesn't care for this plan?" asked Horace.

"I don't suppose she does," said the old man with a grin. "I can't imagine anybody liking Ikey, can you? I think he's a hateful devil. He doesn't pay his debts, he has no sense of honour, very little sense of decency; his associates, including myself, are the worst men in London."

He shook his head suspiciously.

"He's being virtuous now," he growled, "told me so confidentially; informed me that he was turning over a new leaf. What a rotten confession for a man of his calibre to make! I mistrust him in his penitent mood."

He looked up suddenly.

"You go and cut him out," he said, the tiny flame of malice, which gave his face such an extraordinary character, shining in his eyes. "Good idea, that! Go and cut him out; it struck me Mary was a little keen on you. Damn Ikey! Go along!"

He pushed the astonished youth from him.

Horace found the girl in the conservatory. He was bubbling over with joy. He had never expected to make so easy a conquest of the old man – so easy that he almost felt frightened. It was as if the Earl of Verlond, with that sardonic humour of his, was devising some method of humiliating him. Impulsively he told her all that had happened.

"I can't believe it," he cried, "he was so ready, so willing. He was brutal, of course, but that was natural."

She looked at him with a little glint of amusement in her eyes.

"I don't think you know uncle," she said quietly.

"But – but – " he stammered.

"Yes, I know," she went on, "everybody thinks they do. They think he's the most horrid old man in the world. Sometimes," she confessed, "I have shared their opinion. I can never understand why he sent poor Con away."

"That was your brother?" he asked.

She nodded. Her eyes grew moist.

"Poor boy," she said softly, "he didn't understand uncle. I didn't then. I sometimes think uncle doesn't understand himself very well," she said with a sad little smile. "Think of the horrid things he says about people – think of the way he makes enemies – "

"And yet, I am ready to believe he is a veritable Gabriel," said Horace fervently. "He is a benefactor of the human race, a king among men, the distributor of great gifts – "

"Don't be silly," she said, and laying her hand on his arm, she led him to the farther end of the big palm court.

Whatever pleasure the old lord brought to Horace, it found no counterpart in his dealings with Sir Isaac.

He alternately patted and kicked him, until the baronet was writhing with rage. The old man seemed to take a malicious pleasure in ruffling the other. That the views he expressed at ten o'clock that night were in absolute contradiction to those that he had put into words at eight o'clock on the same night did not distress him; he would have changed them a dozen times during the course of twenty-four hours if he could have derived any pleasure from so doing.

Sir Isaac was in an evil frame of mind when a servant brought him a note. He looked round for a quiet place in which to read it. He half suspected its origin. But why had Black missed so splendid an opportunity of meeting Lord Verlond? The note would explain, perhaps.

He crossed the room and strolled towards the conservatory, reading the letter carefully. He read it twice, then he folded it up and put it into his pocket; he had occasion to go to that pocket again almost immediately, for he pulled out his watch to see the time.

When he had left the little retreat on his way to the hall, he left behind him a folded slip of paper on the floor.

This an exalted Horace, deliriously happy, discovered on his way back to the card-room. He handed it to Lord Verlond, who, having no scruples, read it – and, reading it in the seclusion of his study, grinned.

A POLICEMAN'S BUSINESS

There was living at Somers Town at that time a little man named Jakobs.

He was a man of some character, albeit an unfortunate person with "something behind him." The something behind him, however, had come short of a lagging. "Carpets" (three months' hard labour) almost innumerable had fallen to his share, but a lagging had never come his way.

A little wizened-faced man, with sharp black eyes, very alert in his manner, very neatly dressed, he conveyed the impression that he was enjoying a day off, but so far as honest work was concerned Jakobs' day was an everlasting one.

Mr Jakobs had been a pensioner of Colonel Black's for some years. During that period of time Willie Jakobs had lived the life of a gentleman. That is to say, he lived in the manner which he thought conformed more readily to the ideal than that which was generally accepted by the wealthier classes.

There were moments when he lived like a lord – again he had his own standard – but these periods occurred at rare intervals, because Willie was naturally abstemious. But he certainly lived like a gentleman, as all Somers Town agreed, for he went to bed at whatsoever hour he chose, arose with such larks as were abroad at the moment, or stayed in bed reading his favourite journal.

A fortunate man was he, never short of a copper for a half-pint of ale, thought no more of spending a shilling on a race than would you or I, was even suspected of taking his breakfast in bed, a veritable hallmark of luxury and affluence by all standards.

To him every Saturday morning came postal orders to the value of two pounds sterling from a benefactor who asked no more than that the recipient should be happy and forget that he ever saw a respected dealer in stocks and shares in the act of rifling a dead man's pockets.

For this William Jakobs had seen.

Willie was a thief, born so, and not without pride in his skilful-fingered ancestry. He had joined the firm of Black and Company less with the object of qualifying for a pension twenty years hence than on the off chance of obtaining an immediate dividend.

He was guarded by the very principles which animated the head of his firm.

There was an obnoxious member of the board – obnoxious to the genial Colonel Black – who had died suddenly. A subsequent inquisition came to the conclusion that he died from syncope: even Willie knew no better. He had stolen quietly into the managing director's office one day in the ordinary course of business, for Master Jakobs stole quietly, but literally and figuratively. He was in search of unconsidered stamps and such loose coinage as might be found in the office of a man notoriously careless in the matter of small change. He had expected to find the room empty, and was momentarily paralysed to see the great Black himself bending over the recumbent figure of a man, busily searching the pockets of a dead man for a letter – for the silent man on the floor had come with his resignation in his pocket and had indiscreetly embodied in this letter his reasons for taking the step. Greatest indiscretion of all, he had revealed the existence of this very compromising document to Colonel Black.

Willie Jakobs knew nothing about the letter – had no subtle explanation for the disordered pocket-book. To his primitive mind Colonel Black was making a search for money: it was, in fact, a stamp-hunt on a large scale, and in his agitation he blurted this belief.

At the subsequent inquest Mr Jakobs did not give evidence. Officially he knew nothing concerning the matter. Instead he retired to his home in Somers Town, a life pensioner subject to a continuation of his reticence. Two years later, one Christmas morning, Mr Jakobs received a very beautiful box of chocolates by post, "with every good wish," from somebody who did not trouble to send his or her name. Mr Jakobs, being no lover of chocolate drops, wondered what it had cost and wished the kindly donor had sent beer.

"Hi, Spot, catch!" said Mr Jakobs, and tossed a specimen of the confectioner's art to his dog, who possessed a sweet tooth.

The dog ate it, wagging his tail, then he stopped wagging his tail and lay down with a shiver – dead.

It was some time before Willie Jakobs realized the connection between the stiff little dog and this bland and ornate Christmas gift.

He tried a chocolate on his landlord's dog, and it died. He experimented on a fellow-lodger's canary, and it died too – he might have destroyed the whole of Somers Town's domestic menagerie but for the timely intervention of his landlord, who gave him in charge for his initial murder. Then the truth came out. The chocolates were poisoned. Willie Jakobs found his photograph in the public Press as the hero of a poisoning mystery: an embarrassment for Willie, who was promptly recognized by a Canning Town tradesman he had once victimized, and was arrested for the second time in a week.

Willie came out of gaol (it was a "carpet") expecting to find an accumulation of one pound postal orders awaiting him. Instead he found one five-pound note and a typewritten letter, on perfectly plain uncompromising paper, to the effect that the sender regretted that further supplies need not be expected.

Willie wrote to Colonel Black, and received in reply a letter in which "Colonel Black could not grasp the contents of yours of the 4th. He has never sent money, and fails to understand why the writer should have expected," etc., etc.

Willie, furious and hurt at the base ingratitude and duplicity of his patron, carried the letter and a story to a solicitor, and the solicitor said one word – "Blackmail!" Here, then, was a disgruntled Willie Jakobs forced to work: to depend upon chance bookings and precarious liftings. Fortunately his right hand had not lost its cunning, nor, for the matter of that, had his left. He "clicked" to good stuff, fenced it with the new man in Eveswell Road (he was lagged eventually because he was only an amateur and gave too much for the stuff), and did well – so well, indeed, that he was inclined to take a mild view of Black's offences.

On the evening of Lord Verlond's dinner party – though, to do him justice, it must be confessed that Jakobs knew nothing of his lordship's plans – he sallied forth on business intent.

He made his way through the tiny court and narrow streets which separated him from Stibbington Street, there turning southwards to the Euston Road, and taking matters leisurely, he made his way to Tottenham Court Road, *en route* to Oxford Street.

Tottenham Court Road, on that particular night, was filled with interested people.

They were interested in shop windows, interested in one another, interested in boarding and alighting from buses. It was an ideal crowd from Jakobs' point of view.

He liked people who concentrated, who fixed their minds on one thing and had no thought for any other. In a sense he was something of a psychologist, and he looked sound to find some opulent person whose powers of concentration might be of service to himself.

Gathered round the steps of an omnibus, impatiently waiting for other passengers to disembark, was a little crowd of people, and Jakobs, with his quick, keen eye, spotted a likely client.

He was a stout man of middle age. His hat was placed at such an angle on his head that the Somers Towner diagnosed him as "canned." He may or may not have been right in his surmise. It is sufficient that he appeared comfortably off, and that not only was his coat of good material, but he had various indications of an ostentatious character testifying to his present affluence.

Willie Jakobs had had no intention of taking a bus ride. I doubt very much whether he changed his plans even now, but certain it is that he began to elbow his way into the little throng which surrounded the bus, by this time surging forward to board it.

He elbowed his way with good effect, for suddenly ceasing his efforts, as though he had remembered some very important engagement, he began to back out. He reached the outskirts of the little knot, then turned to walk briskly away.

At that moment a firm hand dropped on his shoulder in quite a friendly way. He looked round quickly. A tall young man in civilian dress stood behind him.

"Hullo!" said the young man, kindly enough, "aren't you going on?"

"No, Mr Fellowe," he said. "I was going down for a blow, but I remember I left the gas burning at home."

"Let's go back and put it out," said Constable Fellowe, who was on a very special duty that night.

"On second thoughts," said Jakobs reflectively, "I don't think it's worth while. After all, it's one of those penny-in-the slot machines and it can only burn itself out."

"Then come along and see if my gas is burning," said Frank humorously.

He held the other's arm lightly, but when Jakobs attempted to disengage himself he found the pressure on his arm increased.

"What's the game?" he asked innocently. "The same old game," said Frank, with a little smile. "Hullo, Willie, you've dropped something."

He stooped quickly, without releasing his hold, and picked up a pocket-book.

The bus was on the point of moving off as Frank swung round and with a signal stopped the conductor.

"I think some one who has just boarded your bus has lost a pocket-book. I think it is that stoutish gentleman who has just gone inside."

The stoutish gentleman hastily descended to make a public examination of his wardrobe. He discovered himself minus several articles which should, by all laws affecting the right of property, have been upon his person.

Thereafter the matter became a fairly commonplace incident.

"It's a cop," said Willie philosophically. "I didn't see you around, Mr Fellowe."

"I don't suppose you did, yet I'm big enough."

"And ugly enough," added Willie impartially.

Frank smiled.

"You're not much of an authority on beauty, Willie, are you?" he asked jocosely, as they threaded their way through the streets which separated them from the nearest police-station.

"Oh, I don't know," said Willie, " 'andsome is as 'andsome does. Say, Mr Fellowe, why don't the police go after a man like Olloroff? What are they worrying about a little hook like me for – getting my living at great inconvenience, in a manner of speaking. He is a fellow who makes his thousands, and has ruined his hundreds. Can you get him a lagging?"

"In time I hope we shall," said Frank.

"There's a feller!" said Willie. "He baits the poor little clerk – gets him to put up a flyer to buy a million pounds' worth of gold mines. Clerk puts it – pinches the money from the till, not meanin' to be dishonest, in a manner of speakin', but expectin' one day to walk into his boss, covered with fame and diamonds, and say, 'Look at your long-lost Horace!' See what I mean?"

Frank nodded.

" 'Look at your prodigal cashier,' " Jakobs continued, carried away by his imagination. " 'Put your lamps over my shiners, run your hooks over me Astrakhan collar. Master, it is I, thy servant!' "

It was not curious that they should speak of Black. There had been a case in court that day in which a too-credulous client of Black's, who had suffered as a result of that credulity, had sued the colonel for the return of his money, and the case had not been defended.

"I used to work for him," said Mr Jakobs, reminiscently. "Messenger at twenty-nine shillings a week – like bein' messenger at a mortuary."

He looked up at Frank.

"Ever count up the number of Black's friends who've died suddenly?" he asked. "Ever reckon that up? He's a regular jujube tree, he is."

" 'Upas' is the word you want, Willie," said Frank gently.

"You wait till the Four get him," warned Mr Jakobs cheerfully. "They won't half put his light out."

He said no more for a while, then he turned suddenly to Frank.

"Come to think of it, Fellowe," he said, with the gross familiarity of the habitué in dealing with his captor, "this is the third time you've pinched me."

"Come to think of it," admitted Frank cheerfully, "it is."

"Harf a mo'."

Mr Jakobs halted and surveyed the other with a puzzled air.

"He took me in the Tottenham Court Road, he took me in the Charin' Cross Road, an' he apperryhended me in Cheapside."

"You've a wonderful memory," smiled the young man.

"Never on his beat," said Mr Jakobs to himself, "always in plain clothes, an' generally watchin' me – now, why?"

Frank thought a moment.

"Come and have a cup of tea, Willie," he said, "and I will tell you a fairy story."

"I think we shall be gettin' at facts very soon," said Willie, in his best judicial manner.

"I am going to be perfectly frank with you, my friend," said Fellowe, when they were seated in a neighbouring coffee-shop.

"If you don't mind," begged Willie, "I'd rather call you by your surname – I don't want it to get about that I'm a pal of yours."

Frank smiled again. Willie had ever been a source of amusement.

"You have been taken by me three times," he said, "and this is the first time you have mentioned our friend Black. I think I can say that if you had mentioned him before it might have made a lot of difference to you, Willie."

Mr Jakobs addressed the ceiling.

"Come to think of it," he said, "he 'inted at this once before."

"I 'int at it once again," said Frank. "Will you tell me why Black pays you two pounds a week?"

"Because he don't," said Willie promptly. "Because he's a sneakin' hook an' because he's a twister, because he's a liar – "

"If there's any reason you haven't mentioned, give it a run," said Constable Fellowe in the vernacular.

Willie hesitated.

"What's the good of my tellin' you?" he asked. "Sure as death you'll tell me I'm only lyin'."

"Try me," said Frank, and for an hour they sat talking, policeman and thief.

At the end of that time they went different ways – Frank to the police-station, where he found an irate owner of property awaiting him, and Mr Jakobs, thankfully, yet apprehensively, to his Somers Town home.

His business completed at the station, and a station sergeant alternately annoyed and mystified by the erratic behaviour of a plain-clothes constable, who gave orders with the assurance of an Assistant-Commissioner, Frank found a taxi and drove first to the house of Black, and later (with instructions to the driver to break all the rules laid down for the regulation of traffic) to Hampstead.

May Sandford was expecting the colonel. She stood by the drawing-room fire, buttoning her glove and endeavouring to disguise her pleasure that her sometime friend had called.

"Where are you going?" was his first blunt greeting, and the girl stiffened.

"You have no right to ask in that tone," she said quietly, "but I will tell you. I am going to dinner."

"With whom?"

The colour came to her face, for she was really annoyed.

"With Colonel Black," she said, with an effort to restrain her rising anger.

He nodded.

"I'm afraid I cannot allow you to go," he said coolly.

The girl stared.

"Once and for all, Mr Fellowe," she said with quiet dignity, "you will understand that I am my own mistress. I shall do as I please. You have no right to dictate to me – you have no right whatever" – she stamped her foot angrily – "to say what I may do and what I may not do. I shall go where and with whom I choose."

"You will not go out tonight, at any rate," said Frank grimly.

An angry flush came to her cheeks.

"If I chose to go tonight, I should go tonight," she said.

"Indeed, you will do nothing of the sort." He was quite cool now – master of himself – completely under control.

"I shall be outside this house," he said, "for the rest of the night. If you go out with this man I shall arrest you."

She started and took a step back.

"I shall arrest you," he went on determinedly. "I don't care what happens to me afterwards. I will trump up any charge against you. I will take you to the station, through the streets, and put you in the iron dock as though you were a common thief. I'll do it because I love you," he said passionately, "because you are the biggest thing in the world to me – because I love you better than life, better than you can love yourself, better than any man could love you. And do you know why I will take you to the police-station?" he went on earnestly. "Because you will be safe there, and the women who look after you will allow no dog like this fellow to have communication with you – because he dare not follow you there, whatever else he dare. As for him – "

He turned savagely about as a resplendent Black entered the room.

Black stopped at the sight of the other's face and dropped his hand to his pocket.

"You look out for me," said Frank, and Black's face blanched.

The girl had recovered her speech.

"How dare you – how dare you!" she whispered. "You tell me that you will arrest me. How dare you! And you say you love me!" she said scornfully.

He nodded slowly.

"Yes," he said, quietly enough. "I love you. I love you enough to make you hate me. Can I love you any more than that?"

His voice was bitter, and there was something of helplessness in it too, but the determination that underlay his words could not be mistaken.

He did not leave her until Black had taken his leave, and in his pardonable perturbation he forgot that he intended searching the colonel for a certain green bottle with a glass stopper.

Colonel Black returned to his flat that night to find unmistakable evidence that the apartment had been most systematically searched. There existed, however, no evidence as to how his visitors had gained admission. The doors had been opened, despite the fact that they were fastened by a key which had no duplicate, and with locks that were apparently unpickable. The windows were intact, and no attempt had been made to remove money and valuables from the desk which had been ransacked. The only proof of identity they had left behind was the seal which he found attached to the blotting-pad on his desk.

They had gone methodically to work, dropped a neat round splash of sealing-wax, and had as neatly pressed the seal of the organization upon it. There was no other communication, but in its very simplicity this plain "IV" was a little terrifying. It seemed that the members of the Four defied all his efforts at security, laughed to scorn his patent locks, knew more about his movements than his most intimate friends, and chose their own time for their visitations.

This would have been disconcerting to a man of less character than Black; but Black was one who had lived through a score of years – each year punctuated, at regular intervals, with threats of the most terrible character. He had ever lived in the shadow of reprisal, yet he had never suffered punishment.

It was his most fervent boast that he never lost his temper, that he never did anything in a flurry. Now, perhaps for the first time in his life, he was going to work actuated by a greater consideration than self-interest – a consideration of vengeance.

It made him less careful than he was wont to be. He did not look for shadowers that evening, yet shadowers there had been – not one but many.

TO LINCOLN RACES

Sir Isaac Tramber went to Lincoln in an evil frame of mind. He had reserved a compartment, and cursed his luck when he discovered that his reservation adjoined that of Horace Gresham.

He paced the long platform at King's Cross, waiting for his guests. The Earl of Verlond had promised to go down with him and to bring Lady Mary, and it was no joy to Sir Isaac to observe on the adjoining carriage the label, "Reserved for Mr Horace Gresham and party."

Horace came along about five minutes before the train started. He was as cheerful as the noonday sun, in striking contrast to Sir Isaac, whose night had not been too wisely spent. He nodded carelessly to Sir Isaac's almost imperceptible greeting.

The baronet glanced at his watch and inwardly swore at the old earl and his caprices. It wanted three minutes to the hour at which the train left. His tongue was framing a bitter indictment of the old man when he caught a glimpse of his tall, angular figure striding along the platform.

"Thought we weren't coming, I suppose?" asked the earl, as he made his way to the compartment.

"I say, you thought we weren't coming?" he repeated, as Lady Mary entered the compartment, assisted with awkward solicitude by Sir Isaac.

"Well, I didn't expect you to be late."

"We are not late," said the earl.

He settled himself comfortably in a corner seat – the seat which Sir Isaac had specially arranged for the girl. Friends of his and of the old man who passed nodded. An indiscreet few came up to speak.

"Going up to Lincoln, Lord Verlond?" asked one idle youth.

"No," said the earl sweetly, "I am going to bed with the mumps." He snarled the last word, and the young seeker after information fled.

"You can sit by me, Ikey – leave Mary alone," said the old man sharply. "I want to know all about this horse. I have £150 on this thoroughbred of yours; it is far more important than those fatuous inquiries you intend making of my niece."

"Inquiries?" grumbled Sir Isaac resentfully.

"Inquiries!" repeated the other. "You want to know whether she slept last night; whether she finds it too warm in this carriage; whether she would like a corner seat or a middle seat, her back to the engine or her face to the engine. Leave her alone, leave her alone, Ikey. She'll decide all that. I know her better than you."

He glared, with that amusing glint in his eyes, across at the girl.

"Young Gresham is in the next carriage. Go and tap at the window and bring him out. Go along!"

"He's got some friends there, I think, uncle," said the girl.

"Never mind about his friends," said Verlond irritably. "What the devil does it matter about his friends? Aren't you a friend? Go and tap at the door and bring him out."

Sir Isaac was fuming.

"I don't want him in here," he said loudly. "You seem to forget, Verlond, that if you want to talk about horses, this is the very chap who should know nothing about Timbolino."

"Ach!" said the earl testily, "don't you suppose he knows all there is to be known. What do you think sporting papers are for?"

"Sporting papers can't tell a man what the owner knows," said Sir Isaac importantly.

"They tell me more than he knows," he said. "Your horse was favourite yesterday morning – it isn't favourite any more, Ikey."

"I can't control the investments of silly asses," grumbled Sir Isaac.

"Except one," said the earl rudely. "But these silly asses you refer to do not throw their money away – remember that, Ikey. When you have had as much racing as I have had, and won as much money as I have won, you'll take no notice of what owners think of their horses.

You might as well ask a mother to give a candid opinion of her own daughter's charms as to ask an owner for unbiased information about his own horse."

The train had slipped through the grimy purlieus of London and was now speeding through green fields to Hatfield. It was a glorious spring day, mellow with sunlight: such a day as a man at peace with the world might live with complete enjoyment.

Sir Isaac was not in this happy position, nor was he in a mood to discuss either the probity of racing men or the general question of the sport itself.

He observed with an inward curse the girl rise and walk, apparently carelessly, into the corridor. He could have sworn he heard a tap at the window of the next compartment, but in this, of course, he was wrong. She merely moved across the vision of the little coterie who sat laughing and talking, and in an instant Horace had come out.

"It is not my fault this, really," she greeted him, with a little flush in her cheeks. "It was uncle's idea."

"Your uncle is an admirable old gentleman," said Horace fervently. "I retract anything I may have said to his discredit."

"I will tell him," she said, with mock gravity.

"No, no," cried Horace, "I don't want you to do that exactly."

"I want to talk to you seriously," said she suddenly. "Come into our compartment. Uncle and Sir Isaac are so busy discussing the merits of Timbolino – is that the right name?" He nodded, his lips twitching with amusement.

"That they won't notice anything we have to say," she concluded.

The old earl gave him a curt nod. Sir Isaac only vouchsafed a scowl. It was difficult to maintain anything like a confidential character in their conversation, but by manoeuvring so that they spoke only of the more important things when Sir Isaac and his truculent guest were at the most heated point of their argument, she was able to unburden the anxiety of her mind.

"I am worried about uncle," she said in a low tone.

"Is he ill?" asked Horace.

She shook her head.

"No, it isn't his illness – yet it may be. But he is so contradictory; I am so afraid that it might react to our disadvantage. You know how willing he was that you should…"

She hesitated, and his hand sought hers under the cover of an open newspaper.

"It was marvellous," he whispered, "wasn't it? I never expected for one moment that the old dev – that your dear uncle," he corrected himself, "would have been so amenable."

She nodded again.

"You see," she said, taking advantage of another heated passage between the old man and the irritated baronet, "what he does so impetuously he can undo just as easily. I am so afraid he will turn and rend you."

"Let him try," said Horace. "I am not easily rent."

Their conversation was cut short abruptly by the intervention of the man they were discussing.

"Look here, Gresham," snapped the earl shortly, "you're one of the *cognoscenti*, and I suppose you know everything. Who are the 'Four Just Men' I hear people talking about?"

Horace was conscious of the fact that the eyes of Sir Isaac Tramber were fixed on him curiously. He was a man who made no disguise of his suspicion.

"I know no more than you," said Horace. "They seem to me to be an admirable body of people who go about correcting social evils."

"Who are they to judge what is and what is not evil?" growled the earl, scowling from under his heavy eyebrows. "Infernal cheek!" What do we pay judges and jurymen and coroners and policemen and people of that sort for, eh? What do we pay taxes for, and rent for, and police rates, and gas rates, and water rates, and every kind of dam' rate that the devilish ingenuity of man can devise? Do we do it that these jackanapes can come along and interfere with the course of justice? It's absurd! It's ridiculous!" he stormed.

Horace threw out a protesting hand.

"Don't blame me," he said.

"But you approve of them," accused the earl. "Ikey says you do, and Ikey knows everything – don't you, Ikey?"

Sir Isaac shifted uncomfortably in his seat. "I didn't say Gresham knew anything about it," he began lamely.

"Why do you lie, Ikey; why do you lie?" asked the old man testily. "You just told me that you were perfectly sure that Gresham was one of the leading spirits of the gang."

Sir Isaac, inured as he was to the brutal indiscretions of his friends, went a dull red.

"Oh, I didn't mean that exactly," he said, awkwardly and a little angrily. "Dash it, Lord Verlond, don't embarrass a fellow by rendering him liable to heavy damages and all that sort of thing."

Horace was unperturbed by the other's confusion.

"You needn't bother yourself," he said coolly. "I should never think of taking you to a court of justice."

He turned again to the girl, and the earl claimed the baronet's attention. The old man had a trick of striking off at a tangent; from one subject to another he leapt like a will-o'-the-wisp. Before Horace had framed half a dozen words the old man was dragging his unwilling victim along a piscatorial road, and Sir Isaac was floundering out of his depths in a morass – if the metaphor be excused – of salmon-fishing, trout-poaching, pike-fishing – a sport on which Sir Isaac Tramber could by no means deem himself an authority.

It was soon after lunch that the train pulled into Lincoln. Horace usually rented a house outside the town, but this year he had arranged to go and return to London on the same night. At the station he parted with the girl.

"I shall see you on the course," he said. "What are your arrangements? Do you go back to town tonight?"

She nodded.

"Is this a very important race for you to win?" she asked, a little anxiously.

He shook his head.

"Nobody really bothers overmuch about the Lincolnshire Handicap," he said. "You see, it's too early in the season for even the gamblers to put their money down with any assurance. One doesn't know much, and it is almost impossible to tell what horses are in form. I verily believe that Nemesis will win, but everything is against her.

"You see, the Lincoln," continued Horace doubtfully, "is a race which is not usually won by a filly, and then, too, she is a sprinter. I know sprinters have won the race before, and every year have been confidently expected to win it again; but the averages are all against a horse like Nemesis."

"But I thought," she said in wonder, "that you were so confident about her."

He laughed a little.

"Well, you know, one is awfully confident on Monday and full of doubts on Tuesday. That is part of the game; the form of horses is not half as inconsistent as the form of owners. I shall probably meet a man this morning who will tell me that some horse is an absolute certainty for the last race of the day. He will hold me by the buttonhole and he will drum into me the fact that this is the most extraordinarily easy method of picking up money that was ever invented since racing started. When I meet him after the last race he will coolly inform me that he did not back that horse, but had some tip at the last moment from an obscure individual who knew the owner's aunt's sister. You mustn't expect one to be consistent.

"I still think Nemesis will win," he went on, "but I am not so confident as I was. The most cocksure of students gets a little glum in the face of the examiner."

The earl had joined them and was listening to the conversation with a certain amount of grim amusement.

"Ikey is certain Timbolino will win," he said, "even in the face of the examiner. Somebody has just told me that the examiner is rather soft under foot."

"You mean the course?" asked Horace, a little anxiously.

The earl nodded.

"It won't suit yours, my friend," he said. "A sprinter essaying the Lincolnshire wants good going. I can see myself taking £1,500 back to London today."

"Have you backed Timbolino?"

"Don't ask impertinent questions," said the earl curtly. "And unnecessary questions," he went on. "You know infernally well I've backed Timbolino. Don't you believe me? I've backed it and I'm afraid I'm not going to win."

"Afraid?"

Whatever faults the old man had, Horace knew him for a good loser.

The earl nodded.

He was not amused now. He had dropped like a cloak the assumption of that little unpleasant leering attitude. He was, Horace saw for the first time, a singularly good-looking old man. The firm lines of the mouth were straight, and the pale face, in repose, looked a little sad.

"Yes, I'm afraid." he said. His voice was even and without the bitter quality of cynicism which was his everlasting pose.

"This race makes a lot of difference to some people. It doesn't affect me very much," he said, and the corner of his mouth twitched a little. "But there are people," he went on seriously, "to whom this race makes a difference between life and death." There was a sudden return to his usual abrupt manner. "Eh? How does that strike you for good melodrama, Mr Gresham?"

Horace shook his head in bewilderment.

"I'm afraid I don't follow you at all, Lord Verlond."

"You may follow me in another way," said the earl briskly. "Here is my car. Good morning."

Horace watched him out of sight and then made his way to the racecourse.

The old man had puzzled him not a little. He bore, as Horace knew, a reputation which, if not unsavoury, was at least unpleasant. He was credited with having the most malicious tongue in London. But when Horace came to think, as he did, walking along the banks of the river on his way to the course, there was little that the old man had ever said which would injure or hurt innocent people. His cynicism was in the main directed against his own class, his savageness most manifested against notorious sinners. Men like Sir Isaac Tramber felt the lash of his tongue.

His treatment of his heir was, of course, inexcusable. The earl himself never excused it; he persistently avoided the subject, and it would be a bold man who would dare to raise so unpleasant a topic against the earl's wishes.

He was known to be extraordinarily wealthy, and Horace Gresham had reason for congratulating himself that he had been specially blessed with this world's goods. Otherwise his prospects would not have been of the brightest. That he was himself enormously rich precluded any suggestion (and the suggestion would have been inevitable) that he hunted Lady Mary's fortune. It was a matter of supreme indifference to himself whether she inherited the Verlond millions or whether she came to him empty-handed.

There were other people in Lincoln that day who did not take so philosophical a view of the situation.

Sir Isaac had driven straight to the house on the hill leading to the Minster, which Black had engaged for two days. He was in a very bad temper when at last he reached his destination. Black was sitting at lunch.

Black looked up as the other entered. "Hullo, Ikey," he said, "come and sit down."

Sir Isaac looked at the menu with some disfavour.

"Thanks," he said shortly, "I've lunched on the train. I want to talk to you."

"Talk away," said Black, helping himself to another cutlet. He was a good trencherman – a man who found exquisite enjoyment in his meals.

"Look here, Black," said Isaac, "things are pretty desperate. Unless that infernal horse of mine wins today I shall not know what to do for money."

"I know one thing you won't be able to do," said Black coolly, "and that is, come to me. I am in as great straits as you."

He pushed back his plate and took a cigar case from his pocket.

"What do we stand to win on this Timbolino of yours?"

"About £25,000," said Sir Isaac moodily. "I don't know if the infernal thing will win. It would be just my luck if it doesn't. I am afraid of this horse of Gresham's."

Black laughed softly.

"That's a new fear of yours," he said. "I don't remember having heard it before."

"It's no laughing matter," said the other. "I had my trainer, Tubbs, down watching her work. She is immensely fast. The only thing is whether she can stay the distance."

"Can't she be got at?" asked Black.

"Got at!" said the other impatiently. "The race will be run in three hours' time. Where do you get your idea of racing from?" he asked irritably. "You can't poison horses at three hours' notice. You can't even poison then at three days' notice, unless you've got the trainer in with you. And trainers of that kind only live in novels."

Black was carefully cutting the end of his cigar.

"So if your horse loses we shall be in High Street, Hellboro'?" he reflected. "I have backed it to save my life." He said this in grim earnest.

He rang a bell. The servant came in.

"Tell them to bring round the carriage," he said. He looked at his watch. "I am not particularly keen on racing, but I think I shall enjoy this day in the open. It gives one a chance of thinking."

THE RACE

The curious ring on the Carholme was crowded. Unusually interested in the Lincoln Handicap was the sporting world, and this, together with the glorious weather, had drawn sportsmen from North and South to meet together on this great festival of English racing.

Train and steamer had brought the wanderers back to the fold. There were men with the tan of Egypt on their cheeks, men who had been to the South to avoid the vigorous and searching tests of an English winter; there were men who came from Monte Carlo, and lean, brown men who had spent the dark days of the year amongst the snows of the Alps.

There were regular followers of the game who had known no holiday, and had followed the jumping season with religious attention. There were rich men and comparatively poor men; little tradesmen who found this the most delightful of their holidays; Members of Parliament who had snatched the day from the dreariness of the Parliamentary debates; sharpers on the look-out for possible victims; these latter quiet, unobtrusive men whose eyes were constantly on the move for a likely subject. There was a sprinkling of journalists, cheery and sceptical, young men and old men, farmers in their gaiters – all drawn together in one great brotherhood by a love of the sport of kings.

In the crowded paddock the horses engaged in the first race were walking round, led by diminutive stable-lads, the number of each horse strapped to the boy's arm.

"A rough lot of beggars," said Gresham, looking them over. Most of them still had their winter coats; most of them were grossly fat and unfitted for racing. He was ticking the horses off on his card; some he immediately dismissed as of no account. He found Lady Mary wandering around the paddock by herself. She greeted him as a shipwrecked mariner greets a sail.

"I'm so glad you've come," she said. "I know nothing whatever about racing." She looked round the paddock. "Won't you tell me something. Are all these horses really fit?"

"You evidently know something about horses," he smiled. "No, they're not."

"But surely they can't win if they're not fit," she said in astonishment.

"They can't all win," replied the young man, laughing. "They're not all intended to win, either. You see, a trainer may not be satisfied his horse is top-hole. He sends him out to have a feeler, so to speak, at the opposition. The fittest horse will probably win this race. The trainer who is running against him with no hope of success will discover how near to fitness his own beast is!"

"I want to find Timbolino," she said, looking at her card. "That's Sir Isaac's, isn't it?"

He nodded. "I was looking for him myself," he said. "Come along, and let's see if we can find him."

In a corner of the paddock they discovered the horse – a tall, upstanding animal, well muscled, so far as Horace could judge, for the horse was still in his cloths.

"A nice type of horse for the Lincoln," he said thoughtfully. "I saw him at Ascot last year. I think this is the fellow we've got to beat."

"Does Sir Isaac own many horses?" she asked.

"A few," he said. "He is a remarkable man."

"Why do you say that?" she asked.

He shrugged his shoulders.

"Well, one knows…"

Then he realized that it wasn't playing cricket to speak disparagingly of a possible rival, and she rightly interpreted his silence.

"Where does Sir Isaac make his money?" she asked abruptly.

He looked at her.

"I don't know," he said. "He's got some property somewhere, hasn't he?"

She shook her head.

"No," she said. "I am not asking," she went on quickly, "because I have any possible interest in his wealth or his prospects. All my interest is centred – elsewhere."

She favoured him with a dazzling little smile.

Although the paddock was crowded and the eyes of many people were upon him, the owner of the favourite had all his work to restrain himself from taking her hand.

She changed the subject abruptly.

"So now let's come and see your great horse," she said gaily.

He led her over to one of the boxes where Nemesis was receiving the attention of an earnest groom.

There was not much of her. She was of small build, clean of limb, with a beautiful head and a fine neck not usually seen in so small a thoroughbred. She had run a good fourth in the Cambridgeshire of the previous year, and had made steady improvement from her three-year-old to her four-year-old days.

Horace looked her over critically. His practised eye could see no fault in her condition. She looked very cool, ideally fit for the task of the afternoon. He knew that her task was a difficult one; he knew, too, that he had in his heart really very little fear that she could fail to negotiate the easy mile of the Carholme. There were many horses in the race who were also sprinters, and they would make the pace a terrifically fast one. If stamina was a weak point, it would betray her.

The previous day, on the opening of the racing season, his stable had run a horse in a selling plate, and it was encouraging that this animal, though carrying top weight, beat his field easily. It was this fact that had brought Nemesis to the position of short-priced favourite.

Gresham himself had very little money upon her; he did not bet very heavily, though he was credited with making and losing fabulous sums each year. He gained nothing by contradicting these rumours.

He was sufficiently indifferent to the opinions of his fellows not to suffer any inconvenience from their repetition.

But the shortening of price on Nemesis was a serious matter for the connection of Timbolino. They could not cover their investments by "saving" on Nemesis without a considerable outlay.

Horace was at lunch when the second race was run. He had found Lord Verlond wonderfully gracious; to the young man's surprise his lordship had accepted his invitation with such matter-of-fact heartiness as to suggest he had expected it.

"I suppose," he said, with a little twinkle in his eye, "you haven't invited Ikey?"

Gresham shook his head smilingly.

"No, I do not think Sir Isaac quite approves of me."

"I do not think he does," agreed the other. "Anyway, he's got a guest of his own, Colonel Black. I assure you it is through no act of mine. Ikey introduced him to me, somewhat unnecessarily, but Ikey is always doing unnecessary things.

"A very amiable person," continued the earl, busy with his knife and fork; "he 'lordshipped' me and 'my lorded' me as though he were the newest kind of barrister and I was the oldest and wiliest of assize judges. He treated me with that respect which is only accorded to those who are expected to pay eventually for the privilege. Ikey was most anxious that he should create a good impression."

It may be said with truth that Black saw the net closing round him. He knew not what mysterious influences were at work, but day by day, in a hundred different ways, he found himself thwarted, new obstacles put in his way. He was out now for a final kill.

He was recalled to a realization of the present by the strident voices of the bookmakers about him; the ring was in a turmoil. He heard a voice shout, "Seven to one, bar one! Seven to one Nemesis!" and he knew enough of racing to realize that something had happened to the favourite. He came to a bookmaker he knew slightly.

"What are you barring?" he asked.

"Timbolino," was the reply.

He found Sir Isaac near the enclosure. The baronet was looking a muddy white, and was biting his finger-nails with an air of perturbation.

"What has made your horse so strong a favourite?"

"I backed it again," said Sir Isaac.

"Backed it again?"

"I've got to do something," said the other savagely. "If I lose, well, I lose more than I can pay. I might as well add to my liabilities. I tell you I'm down and out if this thing doesn't win," he said, "unless you can do something for me. You can, can't you, Black, old sport?" he asked entreatingly. "There's no reason why you and I should have any secrets from one another."

Black looked at him steadily. If the horse lost he might be able to use this man to greater advantage.

Sir Isaac's next words suggested that in case of necessity help would be forthcoming.

"It's that beastly Verlond," he said bitterly. "He put the girl quite against me — she treats me as though I were dirt — and I thought I was all right there. I've been backing on the strength of the money coming to me."

"What has happened recently?" asked Black.

"I got her by myself just now," said the baronet, "and put it to her plain; but it's no go, Black, she gave me the frozen face — turned me down proper. It's perfectly damnable," he almost wailed.

Black nodded. At that moment there was a sudden stir in the ring. Over the heads of the crowd from where they stood they saw the bright-coloured caps of the jockeys cantering down to the post.

Unlike Sir Isaac, who had carefully avoided the paddock after a casual glance at his candidate, Horace was personally supervising the finishing touches to Nemesis. He saw the girths strapped and gave his last instructions to the jockey. Then, as the filly was led to the course, with one final backward and approving glance at her, he turned towards the ring.

"One moment, Gresham!" Lord Verlond was behind him. "Do you think your horse," said the old man, with a nod towards Nemesis, "is going to win?"

Horace nodded.

"I do now," he said; "in fact, I am rather confident."

"Do you think," the other asked slowly, "that if your horse doesn't, Timbolino will?"

Horace looked at him curiously.

"Yes, Lord Verlond, I do," he said quietly.

Again there was a pause, the old man fingering his shaven chin absently.

"Suppose, Gresham," he said, without raising his voice, "suppose I asked you to pull your horse?"

The face of the young man went suddenly red.

"You're joking, Lord Verlond," he answered stiffly.

"I'm not joking," said the other. "I'm speaking to you as a man of honour, and I am trusting to your respecting my confidence. Suppose I asked you to pull Nemesis, would you do it?"

"No, frankly, I would not," said the other, "but I can't – "

"Never mind what you can't understand," said Lord Verlond, with a return of his usual sharpness. "If I asked you and offered you as a reward what you desired most, would you do it?"

"I would not do it for anything in the world," said Horace gravely.

A bitter little smile came to the old man's face.

"I see," he said.

"I can't understand why you ask me," said Horace, who was still bewildered. "Surely you – you know – "

"I only know that you think I want you to pull your horse because I have backed the other," said the old earl, with just a ghost of a smile on his thin lips. "I would advise you not to be too puffed up with pride at your own rectitude," he said unpleasantly, though the little smile still lingered, "because you may be very sorry one of these days that you did not do as I asked."

"If you would tell me," began Horace, and paused. This sudden request from the earl, who was, with all his faults, a sportsman, left him almost speechless.

"I will tell you nothing," said the earl, "because I have nothing to tell you," he added suavely.

Horace led the way up the stairs to the county stand. To say that he was troubled by the extraordinary request of the old man would be to put it mildly. He knew the earl as an eccentric man; he knew him by reputation as an evil man, though he had no evidence as to this. But he never in his wildest and most uncharitable moments had imagined that this old rascal – so he called him – would ask him to pull a horse. It was unthinkable. He remembered that Lord Verlond was steward of one or two big meetings, and that he was a member of one of the most august sporting clubs in the world.

He elbowed his way along the top of the stand to where the white osprey on Lady Mary's hat showed.

"You look troubled," she said as he reached her side. "Has uncle been bothering you?"

He shook his head. "No," he replied, with unusual curtness.

"Has your horse developed a headache?" she asked banteringly.

"I was worried about something I remembered," he said incoherently.

The field was at the starting-post.

"Your horse is drawn in the middle," she said.

He put up his glasses. He could see the chocolate and green plainly enough.

Sir Isaac's – grey vertical stripes on white, yellow cap – was also easy to see. He had drawn the inside right.

The field was giving the starter all the trouble that twenty-four high-spirited thoroughbreds could give to any man. For ten minutes they backed and sidled and jumped and kicked and circled before the two long tapes. With exemplary patience the starter waited, directing, imploring almost, commanding and, it must be confessed, swearing, for he was a North-country starter who had no respect for the cracks of the jockey world.

The wait gave Horace an opportunity for collecting his thoughts. He had been a little upset by the strange request of the man who was now speaking so calmly at his elbow.

For Sir Isaac the period of waiting had increased the tension. His hands were shaking, his glasses went up and down, jerkily; he was in an agony of apprehension, when suddenly the white tape swung up, the field bunched into three sections, then spread again and, like a cavalry regiment, came thundering down the slight declivity on its homeward journey.

"They're off!"

A roar of voices. Every glass was focused on the oncoming field. There was nothing in it for two furlongs; the start had been a splendid one. They came almost in a dead line. Then something on the rail shot out a little: it was Timbolino, going with splendid smoothness.

"That looks like the winner," said Horace philosophically. "Mine's shut in."

In the middle of the course the jockey on Nemesis, seeking an opening, had dashed his mount to one which was impossible.

He found himself boxed between two horses, the riders of which showed no disposition to open out for him. The field was half-way on its journey when the boy pulled the filly out of the trap and "came round his horses."

Timbolino had a two-length clear lead of Colette, which was a length clear of a bunch of five; Nemesis, when half the journey was done, was lying eighth or ninth.

Horace, on the stand, had his stop-watch in his hand. He clicked it off as the field passed the four-furlong post and hastily examined the dial.

"It's a slow race," he said, with a little thrill in his voice.

At the distance, Nemesis, with a quick free stride, had shot out of the ruck and was third, three lengths behind Timbolino.

The boy on Sir Isaac's horse was riding a confident race. He had the rails and had not moved on his horse. He looked round to see where the danger lay, and his experienced eye saw it in Nemesis, who was going smoothly and evenly.

A hundred yards from the post the boy on Gresham's filly shook her up, and in half a dozen strides she had drawn abreast of the leader.

The rider of Timbolino saw the danger – he pushed his mount, working with hands and heels upon the willing animal under him.

They were running now wide of each other, dead level. The advantage, it seemed, lay with the horse on the rails, but Horace, watching with an expert eye from the top of the stand, knew that the real advantage lay with the horse in the middle of the track.

He had walked over the course that morning, and he knew that it was on the crown of the track that the going was best. Timbolino responded nobly to the efforts of his rider; once his head got in front, and the boy on Nemesis took up his whip, but he did not use it. He was watching the other. Then, with twenty yards to go, he drove Nemesis forward with all the power of his splendid hands.

Timbolino made one more effort, and as they flew past the judge's box there was none save the judge who might separate them.

Horace turned to the girl at his side with a critical smile.

"Oh, you've won," she said. "You did win, didn't you?"

Her eyes were blazing with excitement.

He shook his head smilingly.

"I'm afraid I can't answer that," he said. "It was a very close thing."

He glanced at Sir Isaac. The baronet's face was livid, the hand that he raised to his lips trembled like an aspen leaf.

"There's one man," thought Horace, "who's more worried about the result than I am."

Down below in the ring there was a Babel of excited talk. It rose up to them in a dull roar. They were betting fast and furiously on the result, for the numbers had not yet gone up.

Both horses had their partisans. Then there was a din amounting to a bellow. The judge had hoisted two noughts in the frame. It was a dead-heat!

"By Jove!" said Horace.

It was the only comment he made.

He crossed to the other side of the enclosure as quickly as he could, Sir Isaac following closely behind. As the baronet elbowed his way through the crowd somebody caught him by the arm. He looked round. It was Black.

"Run it off," said Black, in a hoarse whisper. "It was a fluke that horse got up. Your jockey was caught napping. Run it off."

Sir Isaac hesitated.

"I shall get half the bets and half the stakes," he said.

"Have the lot," said Black. "Go along, there is nothing to be afraid of. I know this game; run it off. There's nothing to prevent you winning."

Sir Isaac hesitated, then walked slowly to the unsaddling enclosure. The steaming horses were being divested of their saddles.

Gresham was there, looking cool and cheerful. He caught the baronet's eye.

"Well, Sir Isaac," he said pleasantly, "what are you going to do?"

"What do you want to do?" asked Sir Isaac suspiciously.

It was part of his creed that all men were rogues. He thought it would be safest to do the opposite to what his rival desired. Like many another suspicious man, he made frequent errors in his diagnosis.

"I think it would be advisable to divide," said Horace. "The horses have had a very hard race, and I think mine was unlucky not to win."

That decided Sir Isaac.

"We'll run it off," he said.

"As you will," said Horace coldly, "but I think it is only right to warn you that my horse was boxed in half-way up the course and but for that would have won very easily. He had to make up half a dozen—"

"I know all about that," interrupted the other rudely, "but none the less, I'm going to run it off."

Horace nodded. He turned to consult with his trainer. If the baronet decided to run the dead-heat off, there was nothing to prevent it, the laws of racing being that both owners must agree to divide.

Sir Isaac announced his intention to the stewards, and it was arranged that the runoff would take place after the last race of the day.

He was shaking with excitement when he rejoined Black.

"I'm not so sure that you're right," he said dubiously. "This chap Gresham says his horse was boxed in. I didn't see the beast in the race, so I can't tell. Ask somebody."

"Don't worry," said Black, patting him on the back, "there is nothing to worry about; you'll win this race just as easily as I shall walk from this ring to the paddock."

Sir Isaac was not satisfied. He waited till he saw a journalist whom he knew by sight returning from the telegraph office.

"I say," he said, "did you see the race?"

The journalist nodded.

"Yes, Sir Isaac," he said with a smile. "I suppose Gresham insisted on running it off?"

"No, he didn't," said Sir Isaac, "but I think I was unlucky to lose."

The journalist made a little grimace.

"I'm sorry I can't agree with you," he said. "I thought that Mr Gresham's horse ought to have won easily, but that he was boxed in the straight."

Sir Isaac reported this conversation to Black.

"Take no notice of these racing journalists," said Black contemptuously. "What do they know? Haven't I got eyes as well as they?"

But this did not satisfy Sir Isaac.

"These chaps are jolly good judges," he said. "I wish to heaven I had divided."

Black slapped him on the shoulder.

"You're losing your nerve, Ikey," he said. "Why, you'll be thanking me at dinner tonight for having saved you thousands of pounds. He didn't want to run it off?"

"Who?" asked Sir Isaac. "Gresham?"

"Yes; did he?" asked Black.

"No, he wasn't very keen. He said it wasn't fair to the horses."

Black laughed.

"Rubbish!" he said scornfully. "Do you imagine a man like that cares whether his horse is hard raced or whether it isn't? No! He saw the race as well as I did. He saw that your fool of a jockey had it won and was caught napping. Of course he didn't want to risk a run-off. I tell you that Timbolino will win easily."

Somewhat reassured by his companion's optimism, Sir Isaac awaited the conclusion of the run-off in better spirits. It added to his assurance that the ring took a similar view to that which Black held. They were asking for odds about Timbolino. You might have got two to one against Nemesis.

But only for a little while.

Gresham had gone into the tea-room with the girl, and was standing at the narrow entrance of the county stand, when the cry, "Two to one Nemesis!" caught his ear.

"They're not laying against my horse!" he exclaimed in astonishment.

He beckoned a man who was passing.

"Are they laying against Nemesis?" he asked.

The man nodded. He was a commission agent, who did whatever work the young owner required.

"Go in and back her for me. Put in as much money as you possibly can get. Back it down to evens," said Gresham decidedly.

He was not a gambling man. He was shrewd and business-like in all his transactions, and he could read a race. He knew exactly what had happened. His money created some sensation in a market which was not over-strong. Timbolino went out, and Nemesis was a shade odds on.

Then it was that money came in for Sir Isaac's horse.

Black did not bet to any extent, but he saw a chance of making easy money. The man honestly believed all he had said to Sir Isaac. He was confident in his mind that the jockey had ridden a "jolly race." He had sufficient credit amongst the best men in the ring to invest fairly heavily.

Again the market experienced an extraordinary change.

Timbolino was favourite again. Nemesis went out – first six to four, then two to one, then five to two.

But now the money began to come in from the country. The results of the race and its description had been published in the stop press editions in hundreds of evening papers up and down England, Ireland and Scotland.

Quick to make their decisions, the little punters of Great Britain were re-investing – some to save their stakes, others to increase what they already regarded as their winnings.

And here the money was for Nemesis. The reporters, unprejudiced, had no other interest but to secure for the public accurate news and to describe things as they saw them. And the race as they saw it was the race which Sir Isaac would not believe and at which Black openly scoffed.

The last event was set for half-past four, and after the field had come past the post, and the winner was being led to the unsaddling enclosure, the two dead-heaters of the memorable Lincolnshire Handicap came prancing from the paddock on to the course.

The question of the draw was immaterial. There was nothing to choose between the jockeys, two experienced horsemen, and there was little delay at the post. It does not follow that a race of two runners means an equable start, though it seemed that nothing was likely to interfere with the tiny field getting off together. When the tapes went up, however, Nemesis half-turned and lost a couple of lengths.

"I'll back Timbolino," yelled somebody from the ring, and a quick staccato voice cried, "I'll take three to one."

A chorus of acceptances met the offer.

Sir Isaac was watching the race from the public stand. Black was at his side.

"What did I tell you?" asked the latter exultantly. "The money is in your pocket, Ikey, my boy. Look, three lengths in front. You'll win at a walk."

The boy on Nemesis had her well balanced. He did not drive her out. He seemed content to wait those three lengths in the rear. Gresham, watching them through his glasses, nodded his approval.

"They're going no pace," he said to the man at his side. "She was farther behind at this point in the race itself."

Both horses were running smoothly. At the five-furlong post the lad on Nemesis let the filly out just a little. Without any apparent effort she improved her position. The jockey knew now exactly what were his resources and he was content to wait behind. The rest of the race needs very little description. It was a procession until they had reached the distance. Then the boy on Timbolino looked round.

"He's beaten," said Gresham, half to himself. He knew that some jockeys looked round when they felt their mount failing under them.

Two hundred yards from the post Nemesis, with scarcely an effort, drew level with the leader. Out came the other jockey's whip.

One, two, he landed his mount, and the horse went ahead till he was a neck in front. Then, coming up with one long run, Nemesis first drew up, then passed the fast-stopping Timbolino, and won with consummate ease by a length and a half.

Sir Isaac could not believe his eyes. He gasped, dropped his glasses, and stared at the horses in amazement.

It was obvious that he was beaten long before the winning-post was reached.

"He's pulling the horse," he cried, beside himself with rage and chagrin. "Look at him! I'll have him before the stewards. He is not riding the horse!"

Black's hand closed on his arm.

"Drop it, you fool," he muttered. "Are you going to give away the fact that you are broke to the world before all these people? You're beaten fairly enough. I've lost as much as you have. Get out of this."

Sir Isaac Tramber went down the stairs of the grandstand in the midst of a throng of people, all talking at once in different keys. He was dazed. He was more like a man in a dream. He could not realize what it meant to him. He was stunned, bewildered. All that he knew was that Timbolino had lost. He had a vague idea at the back of his mind that he was a ruined man, and only a faint ray of hope that Black would in some mysterious way get him out of his trouble.

"The horse was pulled," he repeated dully. "He couldn't have lost. Black, wasn't it pulled?

"Shut up," snarled the other. "You're going to get yourself into pretty bad trouble unless you control that tongue of yours." He got the shaking man away from the course and put a stiff glass of brandy and water in his hand. The baronet awoke to his tragic position.

"I can't pay, Black," he wailed. "I can't pay – what an awful business for me. What a fool I was to take your advice – what a fool! Curse you, you were standing in with Gresham. Why did you advise me? What did you make out of it?"

"Dry up," said Black shortly. "You're like a babe, Ikey. What are you worrying about? I've told you I've lost as much money as you. Now we've got to sit down and think out a plan for making money. What have you lost?"

Sir Isaac shook his head weakly.

"I don't know," he said listlessly. "Six or seven thousand pounds. I haven't got six or seven thousand pence," he added plaintively. "It's a pretty bad business for me, Black. A man in my position – I shall have to sell off my horses

"Your position!" Black laughed harshly. "My dear good chap, I shouldn't let that worry you."

"Your reputation," he went on. "You're living in a fool's paradise, my man," he said with savage banter. "Why, you've no more reputation than I have. Who cares whether you pay your debts of honour or whether you don't? It would surprise people more if you paid than if you defaulted. Get all that nonsense out of your head and think sensibly. You will make all you've lost and much more. You've got to marry – and quick, and then she's got to inherit my lord's money, almost as quickly."

Ikey looked at him in despairing amazement.

"Even if she married me," he said pettishly, "I should have to wait years for the money."

Colonel Black smiled.

They were moving off the course when they were overtaken by a man, who touched the baronet on the arm.

"Excuse me, Sir Isaac," he said, and handed him an envelope.

"For me?" asked Ikey wonderingly, and opened the envelope. There was no letter – only a slip of paper and four bank-notes for a thousand pounds each.

Sir Isaac gasped and read – "Pay your debts and live cleanly; avoid Black like the devil and work for your living."

The writing was disguised, but the language was obviously Lord Verlond's.

WHO ARE THE FOUR?

Lord Verlond sat at breakfast behind an open copy of The Times. Breakfast was ever an unsociable meal at Verlond House. Lady Mary, in her neat morning dress, was content to read her letters and her papers without expecting conversation from the old man.

He looked across at her. His face was thoughtful. In repose she had always thought it rather fine, and now his grave eyes were watching her with an expression she did not remember having seen before.

"Mary," he asked abruptly, "are you prepared for a shock?"

She smiled, though somewhat uneasily. These shocks were often literal facts.

"I think I can survive it," she said.

There was a long pause, during which his eyes did not leave her face.

"Would you be startled to know that that young demon of a brother of yours is still alive?

"Alive!" she exclaimed, starting to her feet.

There was no need for the old man to ask exactly how she viewed the news. Her face was flushed with pleasure – joy shone in her eyes.

"Oh, is it really true?" she cried.

"It's true enough," said the old man moodily. "Very curious how things turn out. I thought the young beggar was dead, didn't you?"

"Oh, don't talk like that, uncle, you don't mean it."

"I mean it all right," snapped the earl. "Why shouldn't I? He was infernally rude to me. Do you know what he called me before he left?"

"But that was sixteen years ago," said the girl.

"Sixteen grandmothers," said the old man. "It doesn't make any difference to me if it was sixteen hundred years – he still said it. He called me a tiresome old bore – what do you think of that?"

She laughed, and a responsive gleam came to the old man's face.

"It's all very well for you to laugh," he said, "but it's rather a serious business for a member of the House of Lords to be called a tiresome old bore by a youthful Etonian. Naturally, remembering his parting words and the fact that he had gone to America, added to the very important fact that I am a Churchman and a regular subscriber to Church institutions, I thought he was dead. After all, one expects some reward from an All-wise Providence."

"Where is he?" she asked.

"I don't know," said the earl. "I traced him to Texas – apparently he was on a farm there until he was twenty-one. After that his movements seem to have been somewhat difficult to trace."

"Why," she said suddenly, pointing an accusing finger at him, "you've been trying to trace him."

For a fraction of a second the old man looked confused.

"I've done nothing of the sort," he snarled. "Do you think I'd spend my money to trace a rascal who – "

"Oh, you have," she went on. "I know you have. Why do you pretend to be such an awful old man?"

"Anyway, I think he's found out," he complained. "It takes away a great deal of the fortune which would have come to you. I don't suppose Gresham will want you now."

She smiled. He rose from the table and went to the door.

"Tell that infernal villain – "

"Which one?"

"James," he replied, that I'm not to be disturbed. I'm going to my study. I'm not to be disturbed by anyone for any reason; do you understand?"

If it was a busy morning for his lordship, it was no less so for Black and his friend, for it was Monday, and settling day, and in numerous clubs in London expectant bookmakers, in whose volumes the names of Black and Sir Isaac were freely inscribed, examined their watches with feelings that bordered upon apprehension.

But, to the surprise of everybody who knew the men, the settlements were made.

An accession of wealth had come to the "firm."

Sir Isaac Tramber spent that afternoon pleasantly. He was raised from the depths of despair to the heights of exaltation. His debts of honour were paid; he felt it was possible for him to look the world in the face. As a taxi drove him swiftly to Black's office, he was whistling gaily, and smiling at the politely veiled surprise of one of his suspicious bookmakers.

The big man was not at his office, and Sir Isaac, who had taken the precaution of instructing his driver to wait, re-directed him to the Chelsea flat.

Black was dressing for dinner when Sir Isaac arrived.

"Hullo!" he said, motioning him to a seat. You're the man I want. I've got a piece of information that will please you. You are the sort of chap who is scared by these 'Four Just Men.' Well, you needn't be any more. I've found out all about them. It's cost me £200 to make the discovery, but it's worth every penny."

He looked at a sheet of paper lying before him.

"Here is the list of their names. A curious collection, eh? You wouldn't suspect a Wesleyan of taking such steps as these chaps have taken. A bank manager in South London – Mr Charles Grimburd – you've heard of him: he's the art connoisseur, an unexpected person, eh? And Wilkinson Despard – he's the fellow I suspected most of all. I've been watching the papers very carefully. The *Post Herald*, the journal he writes for, has always been very well informed upon these outrages of the Four. They seem to know more about it than any other paper, and then, in addition, this man Despard has been writing pretty vigorously on social problems. He's got a place in Jermyn Street. I put a man on to straighten his servant, who had been betting. He had lost money. My man has been at him for a couple of weeks. There they are." He tossed the sheet across. "Less awe inspiring than when they stick to their masks and their funny titles."

Sir Isaac studied the list with interest.

"But there are only three here," he said. "Who is the fourth?"

" 'The fourth is the leader: can't you guess who it is? Gresham, of course."

"Gresham?"

"I haven't any proof," said Black; "it's only surmise. But I would stake all I have in the world that I'm right. He is the very type of man to be in this — to organize it, to arrange the details."

"Are you sure the fourth is Gresham?" asked Sir Isaac again.

"Pretty sure," said Black.

He had finished his dressing and was brushing his dress-coat carefully with a whisk brush.

"Where are you going?" asked Sir Isaac. "I have a little business tonight," replied the other. "I don't think it would interest you very much."

He stopped his brushing. For a moment he seemed deep in thought.

"On consideration," he said slowly, "perhaps it will interest you. Come along to the office with me. Have you dined?"

"No, not yet."

"I'm sorry I can't dine you," said Black. "I have an important engagement after this which is taking all my attention at present. You're not dressed," he continued. "That's good. We're going to a place where people do not as a rule dress for dinner."

Over his own evening suit he drew a long overcoat, which he buttoned to the neck. He selected a soft felt hat from the wardrobe in the room and put it on before the looking glass.

"Now, come along," he said.

It was dusk, and the wind which howled through the deserted street justified the wrapping he had provided. He did not immediately call a cab, but walked until they came to Vauxhall Bridge Road. By this time Sir Isaac's patience and powers of pedestrianism were almost exhausted.

"Oh, Lord!" he said irritably, "this is not the kind of job I like particularly."

"Have a little patience," said Black. "You don't expect me to call cabs in Chelsea and give my directions for half a dozen people to hear. You don't seem to realize, Ikey, that you and I are being very closely watched."

"Well, they could be watching us now," said Sir Isaac with truth.

"They may be, but the chances are that nobody will be near enough when we give directions to the driver as to our exact destination."

Even Sir Isaac did not catch it, so low was the voice of Black instructing the driver.

Through the little pane at the back of the cab Black scrutinized the vehicles following their route.

"I don't think there is anybody after us at present," he said. "It isn't a very important matter, but if the information came to the Four that their plans were being checkmated it might make it rather awkward for us."

The cab passed down the winding road which leads from the Oval to Kennington Green. It threaded a way through the traffic and struck the Camberwell Road. Half-way down, Black put out his head, and the cab turned sharply to the left. Then he tapped at the window and it stopped.

He got out, followed by Sir Isaac.

"Just wait for me at the end of the street," he said to the driver.

He handed the man some money as a guarantee of his *bona fides*, and the two moved off. The street was one of very poor artisan houses, and Black had recourse to an electric lamp which he carried in his pocket to discover the number he wanted. At last he came to a small house with a tiny patch of garden in front and knocked.

A little girl opened the door.

"Is Mr Farmer in?" said Black.

"Yes, sir," said the little girl, "will you go up?"

She led the way up the carpeted stairs and knocked at a small door on the left. A voice bade them come in. The two men entered. Seated by the table in a poorly-furnished room, lit only by the fire, was a man. He rose as they entered.

"I must explain," said Black, "that Mr Farmer has rented this room for a couple of weeks. He only comes here occasionally to meet his friends. This," he went on, motioning to Sir Isaac, "is a great friend of mine."

He closed the door, and waited till the little girl's footsteps on the stairs had died away.

"The advantage of meeting in this kind of house," said the man called Farmer, "is that the slightest movement shakes the edifice from roof to basement."

He spoke with what might be described as a "mock-culture" voice. It was the voice of a common man who had been much in the company of gentlemen, and who endeavoured to imitate their intonation without attempting to acquire their vocabulary.

"You can speak freely, Mr Farmer," said Black. "This gentleman is in my confidence. We are both interested in this ridiculous organization. I understand you have now left Mr Wilkinson Despard's employment?"

The man nodded.

"Yes, sir," he said, with a little embarrassed cough. "I left him yesterday."

"Now, have you found out who the fourth is?

The man hesitated.

"I am not sure, sir. It is only fair to tell you that I am not absolutely certain. But I think you could gamble on the fact that the fourth gentleman is Mr Horace Gresham."

"You didn't say that," said Black, "until I suggested the name myself."

The man did not flinch at the suspicion involved in the comment. His voice was even as he replied:

"That I admit, sir. But the other three gentlemen I knew. I had nothing to do with the fourth. He used to come to Mr Despard's late at night, and I admitted him. I never saw his face and never heard his voice. He went straight to Mr Despard's study, and if you knew how the house was portioned out you would realize that it was next to impossible to hear anything!"

"How did you come to know that these men were the Four?" asked Black.

"Well, sir," said the other, obviously ill at ease, "by the way servants generally find things out – I listened."

"And yet you never found out who the leader was?

"No, sir."

"Have you discovered anything else of which I am not aware?"

"Yes, sir," said the man eagerly. "I discovered before I left Mr Despard's employ that they've got you set. That's an old army term which means that they've marked you down for punishment."

"Oh, they have, have they?" said Black. "I overheard that last night. You see, the meeting generally consisted of four. The fourth very seldom turned up unless there was something to do. But he was always the leading spirit. It was he who found the money when money was necessary. It was he who directed the Four to their various occupations. And it was he who invariably chose the people who had to be punished. He has chosen you, I know, sir. They had a meeting the night before last. They were discussing various people, and I heard your name."

"How could you hear?"

"I was in the next room, sir. There's a dressing-room leading out of Mr Despard's room, where these conferences were held. I had a duplicate key."

Black rose as if to go.

"It almost seems a pity you have left that Johnnie. Did they ever speak about me?" asked Sir Isaac, who had been an attentive listener.

"I don't know your name, sir," said the servant deferentially.

"No, and you jolly well won't," answered the baronet promptly.

"I hope, gentlemen," said the man, "that now I have lost my employment you'll do whatever you can to find me another place. If either of you gentlemen want a reliable man-servant – "

He looked inquiringly at Sir Isaac, as being the more likely of the two.

"Not me," said the other brutally. "I find all my work cut out to keep my own secrets, without having any dam' eavesdropping man on the premises to spy on me."

The man against whom this was directed did not seem particularly hurt by the bluntness of the other. He merely bowed his head and made no reply.

Black took a flat case from his inside pocket, opened it and extracted two notes.

"Here are twenty pounds," he said, "which makes £220 you have had from me. Now, if you can find out anything else worth knowing I don't mind making it up to £300 – but it has got to be something good. Keep in with the servants. You know the rest of them. Is there any reason why you shouldn't go back to the flat?"

"No, sir," said the man. "I was merely discharged for carelessness."

"Very good," said Black. "You know my address and where to find me. If anything turns up let me know."

"Yes, sir."

"By the way," said Black, as he made a move to go, "do the Four contemplate taking any action in the immediate future?

"No, sir," said the man eagerly. "I am particularly sure of that. I heard them discussing the advisability of parting. One gentleman wanted to go to the Continent for a month, and another wanted to go to America to see about his mining property. By the way, they all agreed there was no necessity to meet for a month. I gathered that for the time being they were doing nothing."

"Excellent!" said Black.

He shook hands with the servant and departed.

"Pretty beastly sort of man to have about the house," said Sir Isaac as they walked back to the cab.

"Yes," said Black, good-humouredly, "but it isn't my house, and I feel no scruples in the matter. I do not," he added virtuously, "approve of tapping servants for information about their masters and mistresses, but there are occasions when this line of conduct is perfectly justified."

WILLIE JAKOBS TELLS

Left alone, the man whom they had called Farmer waited a few minutes. Then he took down his coat, which hung behind the door, put on his hat and gloves deliberately and thoughtfully, and left the house.

He walked in the direction which Black and Sir Isaac had taken, but their taxi-cab was flying northward long before he reached the spot where it had waited.

He pursued his way into the Camberwell Road and boarded a tram-car. The street lamps and the lights in the shop windows revealed him to be a good-looking man, a little above the average height, with a pale refined face. He was dressed quietly, but well.

He alighted near the Elephant and Castle and strode rapidly along the New Kent Road, turning into one of the poorer streets which lead to a labyrinth of smaller and more poverty-stricken thoroughfares in that district which is bounded on the west by East Street and on the east by the New Kent Road. A little way along, some of the old houses had been pulled down and new buildings in yellow brick had been erected. A big red lamp outside a broad entrance notified the neighbourhood that this was the free dispensary, though none who lived within a radius of five miles needed any information as to the existence of this institution.

In the hallway was a board containing the names of three doctors, and against them a little sliding panel, which enabled them to inform their visitors whether they were in or out. He paused before the board.

The little indicator against the first name said "Out."

Farmer put up his hand and slid the panel along to show the word "In." Then he passed through the door, through the large waiting-room into a small room, which bore the name "Dr Wilson Graille."

He closed the door behind him and slipped a catch. He took off his hat and coat and hung them up. Then he touched a bell, and a servant appeared.

"Is Dr O'Hara in?" he asked.

"Yes, doctor," replied the man.

"Ask him to come along to me, will you, please?"

In a few minutes a man of middle height, but powerfully built, came in and closed the door behind him.

"Well, how did you get on," he inquired, and, uninvited, drew up a chair to the table.

"They jumped at the bait," said Gonsalez with a little laugh. "I think they have got something on. They were most anxious to know whether we were moving at all. You had better notify Manfred. We'll have a meeting tonight. What about Despard? Do you think he would object to having his name used?"

His voice lacked the mock culture which had so deceived Black.

"Not a bit. I chose him purposely because I knew he was going abroad tonight."

"And the others?"

"With the exception of the art man, they are non-existent."

"Suppose he investigates?"

"Not he. He will be satisfied to take the most prominent of the four – Despard, and the other chap whose name I have forgotten. Despard leaves tonight, and the other on Wednesday for America. You see, that fits in with what I told Black."

He took from his pocket the two ten pound notes and laid them on the table.

"Twenty pounds," he said, and handed them to the other man. "You ought to be able to do something with that."

The other stuffed them into his waistcoat pocket.

"I shall send those two Brady children to the seaside," he said. "It probably won't save their lives, but it will give the little devils some conception of what joy life holds – for a month or so."

The same thought seemed to occur to both, and they laughed.

"Black would not like to know to what base use his good money is being put," said Graille, or Farmer, or Gonsalez – call him what you will – with a twinkle in his blue eyes.

"Were they anxious to know who was the fourth man?" asked Poiccart.

"Most keen on it," he said. "But I wondered if they would have believed me if I had confessed myself to be one of the four, and had I at the same time confessed that I was as much in the dark as to the identity of the fourth as they themselves."

Poiccart rose and stood irresolutely, with his hands stuffed into his trousers pockets, looking into the fire.

"I often wonder," he said, "who it is. Don't you?"

"I've got over those sensations of curiosity," said Gonsalez. "Whoever he is, I am of course satisfied that he is a large hearted man, working with a singleness of purpose."

The other nodded in agreement.

"I am sure," said Graille enthusiastically, "that he has done great work, justifiable work, and honourable work."

Poiccart nodded gravely.

"By the way," said the other, "I went to old Lord Verlond – you remember, No. 4 suggested our trying him. He's a pretty bitter sort of person with a sharp tongue."

Poiccart smiled.

"What did he do? Tell you to go to the devil?

"Something of the sort," said Dr Gonsalez. "I only got a grudging half-guinea from him, and he regaled me all the time with more than half a guinea's worth of amusement."

"But it wasn't for this work," said the other.

Gonsalez shook his head.

"No, for another department," he said with a smile.

They had little more time for conversation. Patients began to come in, and within a quarter of an hour the two men were as busy as men could be attending to the injuries, the diseases and the complaints of the people of this overcrowded neighbourhood.

This great dispensary owed its erection and its continuance to the munificence of three doctors who appeared from nowhere. Who the man was who had contributed £5,000 to the upkeep, and who had afterwards appeared in person, masked and cloaked, and had propounded to three earnest workers for humanity his desire to be included in the organization, nobody knew, unless it was Manfred. It was Manfred the wise who accepted not only the offer, but the *bona fides* of the stranger – Manfred who accepted him as a co-partner.

Casual observers described the three earnest medicos not only as cranks, but fanatics. They were attached to no organization; they gave no sign to the world that they could be in any way associated with any of the religious organizations engaged in medical work. It is an indisputable fact that they possessed the qualifications to practise, and that one – Leon Gonsalez – was in addition a brilliant chemist.

No man ever remembered their going to church, or urging attendance at any place of worship. The religious bodies that laboured in the neighbourhood were themselves astonished.

One by one they had nibbled at the sectarian question. Some had asked directly to what religious organization these men were attached. No answer was offered satisfactory to the inquirers.

It was nearly eleven o'clock that night when the work of the two dispensers had finished. The last patient had been dismissed, the last fretful whimper of an ailing child had died away; the door had been locked, the sweepers were engaged in cleaning up the big waiting-room.

The two men sat in the office – tired, but cheerful. The room was well furnished; it was the common room of the three. A bright fire burnt in the fire-place, big roomy armchairs and settees were in evidence. The floor was carpeted thickly, and two or three rare prints hung on the distempered walls.

They were sitting discussing the events of the evening – comparing notes, retailing particulars of interest in cases which had come under their notice. Manfred had gone out earlier in the evening and had not returned.

Then a bell rang shrilly.

Leon looked up at the indicator.

"That is the dispensary door," he said in Spanish. "I suppose we'd better see who it is."

"It will be a small girl," said Poiccart. " 'Please will you come to father; he's either dead or drunk.' "

There was a little laugh at this reminiscence of an incident which had actually happened.

Poiccart opened the door. A man stood in the entrance.

"There's a bad accident just round the corner," he said. "Can I bring him in here, doctor?"

"What sort of an accident?" said Poiccart.

"A man has been knifed."

"Bring him in," said Poiccart.

He went quickly to the common room.

"It's a stabbing case," he said. "Will you have him in your surgery, Leon?"

The young man rose swiftly.

"Yes," he said; "I'll get the table ready."

In a few minutes half a dozen men bore in the unconscious form of the victim. It was a face familiar to the two.

They laid him tenderly upon the surgical table, and with deft hands ripped away the clothing from the wound, whilst the policeman who had accompanied the party pushed back the crowd from the surgery door.

The two men were alone with the unconscious man.

They exchanged glances.

"Unless I am mistaken," said Gonsalez carefully, "this is the late Mr Willie Jakobs."

That evening May Sandford sat alone in her room reading. Her father, when he had come in to say goodbye to May before going to a directors' dinner, had left her ostensibly studying an improving book, but the volume now lay unheeded at her side.

That afternoon she received an urgent note from Black, asking her to meet him "on a matter of the greatest importance." It concerned her father, and it was very secret. She was alarmed, and not a little puzzled. The urgency and the secrecy of the note distressed her unaccountably.

For the twentieth time she began to read the improving plays of Monsieur Moliere, when a knock at the door made her hastily conceal the paper.

"There is a man who wishes to see you," said the girl who had entered in response to her "Come in."

"What sort of man?"

"A common-looking man," said the maid. She hesitated. The butler was in the house, otherwise she would not have seen the visitor.

"Show him into father's study," she said. "Tell Thomas this man is here and ask him to be handy in case I ring for him."

She had never seen the man whom she found waiting. Instinctively she distrusted his face, though there was something about him which compelled her sympathy.

He was white and haggard, black shadows encircled his eyes, and his hands, by no means clean, shook.

"I am sorry to bother you, miss," he said, "but this is important."

"It is rather a late hour," she said. "What is it you want?"

He fumbled with his hat and looked at the waiting girl. At a nod from May she left the room.

"This is rather important to you, miss," said the man again. "Black treated me pretty badly."

For a moment an unworthy suspicion flashed through her mind. Had Frank sent his man to her to shake her faith in Black? A feeling of resentment arose against her visitor and the man she thought was his employer.

"You may save your breath," she said coolly, "and you can go back to the gentleman who sent you and tell him

"Nobody sent me, miss," he said eagerly. "I come on my own. I tell you they've done me a bad turn. I've kept my mouth shut for Black for years, and now he's turned me down. I'm ill, miss, you can see that for yourself," he said, throwing out his arms in despair. "I've been almost starving and they haven't given me a bean. I went to Black's house today and he wouldn't see me."

He almost whimpered in his helpless anger.

"He's done me a bad turn and I'm going to do him one," he said fiercely. "You know what his game is?"

"I do not want to know," she said again, the old suspicion obscuring her vision. "You will gain nothing by speaking against Colonel Black."

"Don't be foolish, miss," he pleaded, "don't think I've come for money. I don't expect money – I don't want it. I dare say I can get help from Mr Fellowe."

"Ah!" she said, "so you know Mr Fellowe: it was he who sent you. I will not hear another word," she went on hotly. "I know now where you come from – I've heard all this before."

She walked determinedly across the room and rang the bell. The butler came in.

"Show this man out," said May.

The man looked at her sorrowfully.

"You've had your chance, miss," he said ominously. "Black's Essley, that's all!"

With this parting shot he shuffled through the hall, down the steps into the night.

Left alone, the girl shrank into her chair. She was shaking from head to foot with indignation and bewilderment. It must have been Frank who sent this man. How mean, how inexpressibly mean!

"How dare he? How dare he?" she asked. It was the policeman in Frank which made him so horrid, she thought. He always believed horrid things of everybody. It was only natural. He had lived his life amongst criminals; he had thought of nothing but breaches of the law.

She looked at the clock: it was a quarter to ten. He had wasted her evening, this visitor. She did not know exactly what to do. She could not read; it was too early to go to bed. She would have liked to have gone for a little walk, but there was nobody to take her. It was absurd asking the butler to walk behind her; she smiled at the thought.

Then she started. She had heard the distant ring of the front-door bell. Who could it be?

She had not long to wait in doubt. A few minutes afterwards the girl had announced Colonel Black. He was in evening dress and very cheerful.

Forgive this visit," he said, with that heartiness of voice which carried conviction of his sincerity. "I happened to be passing and I thought I'd drop in."

This was not exactly true. Black had carefully planned this call. He knew her father was out; knew also, so bitter had been a discussion of that afternoon, that he would not have sanctioned the visit.

May gave him her hand, and he grasped it warmly.

She came straight to the point.

"I'm so glad you've come," she said. "I've been awfully bothered."

He nodded sympathetically, though a little at sea.

"And now this man has come?"

"This man – which man?" he asked sharply.

"I forget his name – he came this evening. In fact, he's only been gone a little time. And he looked awfully ill. You know him, I think?

"Not Jakobs?" he breathed.

She nodded.

"I think that is the name," she said.

"Jakobs?" he repeated, and his face went a little white. "What did he say?" he asked quickly.

She repeated the conversation as nearly as she could remember it. When she had finished he rose.

"You're not going?" she said in astonishment.

"I'm afraid I must," he said. "I've a rather important engagement and – er – I only called in passing. Which way did this man go? Did he give you any idea as to his destination?"

She shook her head.

"No. All that he said was that there were people who would be glad of the information he could give about you."

"He did, did he?" said Black, with an heroic attempt at a smile. "I never thought Jakobs was that kind of man. Of course, there is nothing that I should mind everybody knowing, but one has business secrets, you know, Miss Sandford. He is a discharged employee, of mine who has stolen some contracts. You need not worry about the matter."

He smiled confidently at her as he left the room.

He drove straight from the house to his city office. The place was in darkness, but he knew his way without the necessity of lighting up. He ran upstairs into the boardroom.

There was a little door in one corner of the room, concealed from view by a hanging curtain.

He closed the shutters and pulled down the blinds before he switched on the light. He pushed the curtain aside and examined the face of the door. There was no sign that it had been forced. Jakobs knew of the existence of this little retiring-room, and had, in his indiscretion, mentioned its existence in one of his letters of demand.

Black drew from his pocket a small bunch of keys attached to a silver chain. The door of the room opened easily. There was a smaller room disclosed – no larger than a big cupboard. A single incandescent electric burner slung from the ceiling supplied all the light necessary. There was a dressing table, a chair, a big looking-glass, and a number of hooks from which were suspended a dozen articles of attire. Air was admitted through two ventilators let into the wall and communicating with the main ventilating shaft of the building.

He opened the door of the dressing-table and drew out a number of wigs. They were wigs such as only Fasieur can supply – perfectly modelled and all of one shade of hair, though differently arranged.

He tossed them on to the table impatiently, groping for something which he knew should be there, and was there unless a thief skilled in the use of skeleton keys, and having, moreover, some knowledge of the office, had taken it. He stopped his search suddenly and examined a pad of paper which lay on the table.

It was a pad which he kept handy for note taking – to jot down memoranda. On the white face of the paper was a large brown thumb-mark, and though Colonel Black knew little of the science of anthropology, he was sufficiently well acquainted with the sign to know that it was the mark of a thumb which ought never to have been in this secret office of his.

Then it was Willie! Willie Jakobs, the befriended, the pensioned, and the scorned, who had removed a certain green bottle, the duplicate of which was in his pocket at that moment.

Black did not lose his nerve. He went to a drawer in the desk of his outer office and took out a Browning pistol. It was loaded. He balanced it in his right hand, looked at it reflectively, then put it back again. He hated firearms; they made a great deal of unnecessary noise, and they left behind them too sure an indication of the identity of their user. Men have been traced by bullets.

There were other ways. He lifted from the drawer a long thin knife. It was an Italian stiletto of the sixteenth century – the sort of toy a man might use in these prosaic days for opening his letters. And indeed this was the ostensible reason why Black kept the weapon at hand.

He drew it from its ornate leather sheath and tested its temper, felt its edge and gingerly fingered its point; then he put the stiletto in its case in his overcoat pocket, switched out the light and went out. This was not a case which demanded the employment of the little bottle. There was too little of the precious stuff left, and he had need of it for other purposes.

There were two or three places where he might find the man. A little public house off Regent Street was one. He drove there, stopping the cab a few paces from the spot. He strode into the bar, where men of Jakobs' kind were to be found, but it was empty. The man he sought was not there.

He made a tour of other likely places with no better success. Willie would be at home. He had moved to lodgings on the south side of the Thames.

It was coming from a little public-house off the New Kent Road that Black found his man. Willie had been spending the evening brooding over his grievance, and was on his way home to prepare for his big adventure when Black clapped him on the shoulder.

"Hullo, Willie," he said.

The man turned round with a start.

"Keep your hands off me," he said hastily, stumbling against the wall.

"Now, don't be silly," said Black. "Let's talk this matter out reasonably. You're a reasonable man, aren't you? I've got a cab waiting round the corner."

"You don't get me into no cabs," said Jakobs. "I've had enough of you, Black. You've turned round on me. You cast me out like a dog. Is that the way to treat a pal?"

"You've made a mistake, my friend," said Black smoothly. "We're all liable to make mistakes. I've made many, and I dare say you've made a few. Now, let's talk business."

Willie said nothing. He was still suspicious. Once he thought he saw the other's hand steal to his breast-pocket. He guessed the motive of the action. This, then, was where the bottle was.

Black was an adept in the art of cajolery. He knew the weak places of all the men who had been associated with him. Very slowly he led the other aimlessly, so it seemed, from one street to another until they reached a little cul-de-sac. Stables occupied one side of the tiny street and artisan houses the other. One street-lamp half-way down showed a dim light.

Willie hesitated. "There's no thoroughfare," he said.

"Oh yes, there is," said Black confidently. "I know this neighbourhood rather well. Now, there's one thing I want to ask you, Willie. I'm sure you are feeling more friendly towards me now, aren't you?"

His hand rested almost affectionately on the other's shoulder.

"You didn't play the game," persisted the other.

"Let bygones be bygones," said Black. "What I want to know is, Willie, why did you take the bottle?"

He asked the question in a matter-of-fact tone. He did not raise his voice or give the query unusual emphasis.

The other man was taken off his guard. " 'Well, I felt sore," he said.

"And I suppose," said Black, with gentle reproach, "you're waiting to hand that bottle to our friend Fellowe?"

"I haven't handed it to anybody yet," said Willie, "but to tell you the truth – "

He said no more. The big man's hand suddenly closed round his throat with a grip like steel. Willie struggled, but he was like a child in the grasp of the other.

"You dog," breathed Black.

He shook the helpless man violently. Then with his disengaged hand he whipped the tell-tale phial from the other's pocket and pushed him against the wall.

"And I'll teach you that that's nothing to what you'll get if you ever come across me again."

Jakobs dropped, white and ghastly, against the wall.

"You've got the bottle, Black," he said, "but I know everything that you've done with it."

"You do, do you?"

"Yes, everything," said the other desperately. "You're not going to cast me off, do you hear? You've got to pension me, same as you've done other people. I know enough to send you for a lagging without – "

"I thought you did," said Black.

Something glittered in the light of the lamp, and without a cry Jakobs went down in a huddled heap to the ground.

Black looked round. He wiped the blade of the stiletto carefully on the coat of the stricken man, carefully replaced the weapon in its leather case, and examined his own hands with considerable care for any signs of blood. But these Italian weapons make small wounds.

He turned and, pulling on his gloves, made his way back to where the cab was still waiting.

SIR ISAAC'S FEARS

Under the bright light of a bronze lamp, all that was mortal of Jakobs lay extended upon the operating-table. About the body moved swiftly the shirt-sleeved figures of the doctors.

"I don't think there is much we can do for him," said Gonsalez. "He's had an arterial perforation. It seems to me that he's bleeding internally."

They had made a superficial examination of the wound, and Poiccart had taken so serious a view of the man's condition that he had dispatched a messenger for a magistrate.

Willie was conscious during the examination, but he was too weak and too exhausted to give any account of what had happened.

"There's just a chance," said Gonsalez, "if we could get a JP up in time, that we could give him sufficient strychnine to enable him to tell us who had done this."

"It's murder, I think," said Gonsalez, "the cut's a clean one. Look, there's hardly half an inch of wound. The man who did this used a stiletto, I should say, and used it pretty scientifically. It's a wonder he wasn't killed on the spot."

The hastily-summoned justice of the peace appeared on the scene much sooner than they had anticipated. Gonsalez explained the condition of the man.

"He tried to tell me, after we had got him on the table, who had done it," he said, "but I couldn't catch the name."

"Do you know him?" asked the JP.

"I know him," he said, "and I've rather an idea as to who has done it, but I can't give any reasons for my suspicions."

Jakobs was unconscious, and Gonsalez seized the first opportunity that presented itself of consulting with his colleague.

"I believe this is Black's work," he said hurriedly. "Why not send for him? We know Jakobs has been in his employ and was pensioned by him, and that's sufficient excuse. Possibly, if we can get him down before this poor chap dies, we shall learn something."

"I'll get on the telephone," said the other. He drew from his pocket a memorandum book and consulted its pages. Black's movements and his resorts were fairly well tabulated, but the telephone failed to connect the man they wanted.

At a quarter to two in the morning Jakobs died, without having regained consciousness, and it looked as though yet another mystery had been added to a list which was already appallingly large.

The news came to May Sandford that afternoon. The tragedy had occurred too late that night to secure descriptions in the morning papers; but from the earlier editions of the afternoon journals she read with a shock of the man's terrible fate.

It was only by accident that she learnt of it from this source, for she was still reading of his death in the paper when Black, ostentatiously agitated, called upon her.

"Isn't it dreadful, Miss Sandford?" he said.

He was quite beside himself with grief, the girl thought.

"I shall give evidence, of course, but I shall take great care to keep your name out of it. I think the poor man had very bad associates indeed," he said frankly. "I had to discharge him for that reason. Nobody need know he ever came here," he suggested. "It wouldn't be pleasant for you to be dragged into a sordid case like this."

"Oh, no, no," she said. "I don't want to be mixed up in it at all. I'm awfully sorry, but I can't see how my evidence would help."

"Of course," agreed Black. It had only occurred to him that morning how damning might be the evidence that this girl was in a position to give, and he had come to her in a panic lest she had already volunteered it.

She thought he looked ill and worried, as indeed he was, for Black had slept very little that night. He knew that he was safe from detection. None had seen him meet the man, and although he had visited the resorts which the man frequented, he had not inquired after him.

Yet Black was obsessed by the knowledge that a net was drawing round him. Who were the hunters he could not guess. There came to him at odd moments a strange feeling of terror.

Nothing was going exactly right with him. Sir Isaac had showed signs of revolt.

Before the day was out he found that he had quite enough to bother him without the terrors which the unknown held.

The police had made most strenuous inquiries regarding his whereabouts on the night of the murder. They had even come to him and questioned him with such persistence that he suspected a directing force behind them. He had not bothered overmuch with the "Four Just Men." He had accepted the word of his informant that the Four had separated for the time being, and the fact that Wilkinson Despard had left for America confirmed all that the man had told him.

He was getting short of money again. The settlement of his bets had left him short. Sandford must be "persuaded."

Every day it was getting more and more of a necessity.

One morning Sir Isaac had telephoned him, asking him to meet him in the park.

"Why not come here?" asked Black. "No," said the baronet's voice. "I'd rather meet you in the park."

He named the spot, and at the hour Black met him, a little annoyed that his day's programme should be interrupted by this eccentricity on the part of Sir Isaac Tramber.

The baronet himself did not at once come to the point. He talked around, hummed and hawed, and at last blurted out the truth.

"Look here, Black," he said, "you and I have been good pals – we've been together in some queer adventures, but now I am going to – I want – "

He stammered and spluttered.

"What do you want?" asked Black with a frown.

"Well, to tell the truth," said Sir Isaac, with a pathetic attempt to be firm, "I think it is about time that you and I dissolved partnership."

"What do you mean?" asked Black. "Well, you know, I'm getting talked about," said the other disjointedly. "People are spreading lies about me, and one or two chaps recently have asked me what business you and I are engaged in, and – it's worrying me, Black," he said with the sudden exasperation of a weak man. "I believe I have lost my chance with Verlond because of my association with you."

"I see," said Black.

It was a favourite expression of his. It meant much; it meant more than usual now.

"I understand," he said, "that you think the ship is sinking, and, rat-like, you imagine it is time to swim to the shore."

"Don't be silly, dear old fellow," protested the other, "and don't be unreasonable. You see how it is. When I joined you, you were goin' to do big things – big amalgamations, big trusts, stuffin' an' all that sort of thing. Of course," he admitted apologetically, "I knew all about the bucket shop, but that was a sideline."

Black smiled grimly.

"A pretty profitable sideline for you," he said dryly.

"I know, I know," said Ikey, patient to an offensive degree, "but it wasn't a matter of millions an' all that, now was it?"

Black was thoughtful, biting his nails and looking down at the grass at his feet.

"People are talkin', dear old fellow," Tramber went on, "sayin' the most awful rotten things. You've been promisin' this combination with Sandford's foundries, you've practically issued shares in Amalgamated Foundries of Europe without havin' the goods."

"Sandford won't come in," said Black, without looking up, "unless I pay him a quarter of a million cash – he'll take the rest in shares. I want him to take his price in shares."

"He's no mug," said the baronet coarsely.

"Old Sandford isn't a mug – and I'll bet he's got Verlond behind him. He's no mug either."

143

There was a long and awkward silence – awkward for Sir Isaac, who had an unaccountable desire to bolt.

"So you want to sneak out of it, do you?" said Black, meeting his eyes with a cold smile.

"Now, my dear old chap," said Sir Isaac hastily, "don't take that uncharitable view. Partnerships are always being dissolved, it's what they're for," he said with an attempt at humour. "And I must confess I don't like some of your schemes."

"You don't like!" Black turned round on him with a savage oath. "Do you like the money you've got for it? The money paid in advance for touting new clients? The money given to you to settle your debts at the club? You've got to go through with it, Ikey, and if you don't, I'll tell the whole truth to Verlond and to every pal you've got."

"They wouldn't believe you," said Sir Isaac calmly. "You see, my dear chap, you've got such an awful reputation, and the worst of having a bad reputation is that no one believes you. If it came to a question of believing you or believing me, who do you think Society would believe – a man of some position, one in the baronetage of Great Britain, or a man – well, not to put too fine a point on it – like you?"

Black looked at him long and steadily.

"Whatever view you take," he said slowly, "you've got to stand your corner. If, as a result of any of the business we are now engaged in, I am arrested, I shall give information to the police concerning you. We are both in the same boat – we sink or swim together."

He noticed the slow-spreading alarm on Sir Isaac's face.

"Look here," he said, "I'll arrange to pay you back that money I've got. I'll give you bills – "

Black laughed.

"You're an amusing devil," he said. "You and your bills! I can write bills myself, can't I? I'd as soon take a crossing-sweeper's bills as yours. Why, there's enough of your paper in London to feed Sandford's furnaces for a week."

The words suggested a thought.

"Let's say no more about this matter till after the amalgamation. It's coming off next week. It may make all the difference in our fortune, Ikey," he said in gentler tones. "Just drop the idea of ratting."

"I'm not ratting," protested the other. "I'm merely – "

"I know," said Black. "You're merely taking precautions – well, that's all the rats do. You're in this up to your neck – don't deceive yourself. You can't get out of it until I say 'Go.' "

"It will be awkward for me if the game is exposed," said Sir Isaac, biting his nails. "It will be jolly unpleasant if it is discovered I am standing in with you."

"It will be more awkward for you," answered Black ominously, "if, at the psychological moment, you are *not* standing in with me."

Theodore Sandford, a busy man, thrust his untidy grey head into the door of his daughter's sitting-room.

"May," said he, "don't forget that I am giving a dinner tonight in your honour – for unless my memory is at fault and the cheque you found on your breakfast-tray was missupplied, you are twenty-two today."

She blew him a kiss.

"Who is coming?" she asked. "I ought really to have invited everybody myself."

"Can't stop to tell you," said her father with a smile. "I'm sorry you quarrelled with young Fellowe. I should like to have asked him."

She smiled gaily.

"I shall have to get another policeman," she said.

He looked at her for a long time.

"Fellowe isn't an ordinary policeman," he said quietly. "Do you know that I saw him dining with the Home Secretary the other day?"

Her eyebrows rose.

"In uniform?" she asked.

He laughed.

"No, you goose," he chuckled, "in his dressing-gown."

She followed him down the corridor.

"You've learnt that from Lord Verlond," she said reproachfully.

145

She waited till the car had carried her father from view, then walked back to her room, happy with the happiness which anticipates happiness.

The night before had been a miserable one till, acting on an impulse, she had humbled herself, and found strange joy in the humiliation.

The knowledge that this young man was still her ideal, all she would have him to be, had so absorbed her that for the time being she was oblivious of all else.

She recalled with a little start the occasion of their last meeting, and how they had parted.

The recollection made her supremely miserable again, and, jumping up from her stool, she had opened her little writing-bureau and scribbled a hurried, penitent, autocratic little note, ordering and imploring him to come to her the instant he received it.

Frank came promptly. The maid announced his arrival within ten minutes of Mr Sandford's departure.

May ran lightly downstairs and was seized with a sudden fit of shyness as she reached the library door. She would have paused, but the maid, who was following her, regarded her with so much sympathetic interest that she was obliged to assume a nonchalance that she was far from feeling and enter the room.

Frank was standing with his back to the door, but he turned quickly on hearing the light rustle of her gown.

May closed the door, but she made no effort to move away from it.

"How do you do?" she began.

The effort she was making to still the wild beating of her heart made her voice sound cold and formal.

"I am very well, thank you." Frank's tone reflected her own.

"I – I wanted to see you," she continued, with an effort to appear natural.

"So I gathered from your note," he replied.

"It was good of you to come," she went on conventionally. "I hope it has not inconvenienced you at all."

"Not at all." Again Frank's voice was an expressive echo. "I was just on the point of going out, so came at once."

"Oh, I am sorry – won't you keep your other appointment first? Any time will suit me; it – it is nothing important."

"Well, I hadn't an appointment exactly." It was the young man's turn to hesitate. "To tell the truth, I was coming here."

"Oh, Frank! Were you really?"

"Yes, really and truly, little girl."

May did not answer, but something Frank saw in her face spoke more plainly than words could do.

Mr Sandford returned that afternoon to find two happy people sitting in the half darkness of the drawing-room; and ten members of the Criminal Investigation Department waited at Scotland Yard, alternately swearing and wringing their hands.

COLONEL BLACK MEETS A JUST MAN

Dr Essley's house at Forest Hill stood untenanted. The red lamp before the door was unlit, and though the meagre furnishings had not been removed, the house, with its drawn blinds and grimy steps, had the desolate appearance of emptiness.

The whisper of a rumour had agitated the domestic circles of that respectable suburb – a startling rumour which, if it were true, might well cause Forest Hill to gasp in righteous indignation.

"Dr" Essley was an unauthorized practitioner, a fraud of the worst description, for he had taken the name and the style of a dead man.

"All I know," explained Colonel Black, whom a reporter discovered at his office, "is that I met Dr Essley in Australia, and that I was impressed by his skill. I might say," he added in a burst of frankness, "that I am in a sense responsible for his position in England, for I not only advanced him money to buy his practice, but I recommended him to all my friends, and naturally I am upset by the revelation."

No, he had no idea as to the "doctor's" present location. He had last seen him a month before, when the "doctor" spoke of going to the Continent.

Colonel Black had as much to tell – and no more – to the detectives who came from Scotland Yard. They came with annoying persistence and never seemed tired of coming. They waited for him on the doorstep and in his office. They waited for him in the vestibules of the theatres, at the entrance doors of banks. They came as frequently as emissaries of houses to whom Colonel Black was under monetary obligation.

A week after the events chronicled in the last chapter, Colonel Black sat alone in his flat with a light heart. He had collected together a very considerable amount of money. That it was money to which he had no legal right did not disturb the smooth current of his thoughts. It was sufficient that it was money, and that a motor-car which might carry him swiftly to Folkestone was within telephone-call day and night. Moreover, he was alive.

The vengeance of an organization vowed against Dr Essley had passed over the head of Colonel Black – he might be excused if he thought that the matter of a grey wig and a pair of shaggy eyebrows, added to some knowledge of medicine, had deceived the astute men who had come to England to track him down.

This infernal man Fellowe, who appeared and disappeared as if by magic, puzzled him – almost alarmed him.

Fellowe was not one of the "Four Just Men" – instinct told him that much. Fellowe was an "official."

A Sergeant Gurden who had been extremely useful to Black had been suddenly transferred to a remote division, and nobody knew why. With him had disappeared from his familiar beats a young police constable who had been seen dining with Cabinet Ministers.

It was very evident that there was cause for perturbation – yet, singularly enough, Colonel Black was cheerful; but there was a malignant quality to his cheerfulness. He busied himself with the destruction of such of his papers – and they were few – which he had kept by him.

He turned out an old pocket-book and frowned when he saw its contents. It was a *wagon-lit* coupon for the journey from Paris to Madrid, and was made out in the name of Dr Essley – a mad slip which might have led to serious consequences, he told himself. He burnt the incriminating sheet and crumbled the ashes before he threw them into the fireplace.

It was dark before he had finished his preparations, but he made no attempt to light the room. His dress suit was laid out in an adjoining room, his trunks stood packed.

He looked at his watch. In half an hour he would be on his way to the Sandfords. Here was another risk which none but a madman would take – so he told himself, but he contemplated the outcome of his visit with equanimity.

He went into his bedroom and began his preparations, then remembered that he had left a bundle of notes on his writing-table, and went back. He found the notes and was returning when there was a click, and the room was flooded with light.

He whipped round with an oath, dropping his hand to his hip-pocket.

"Don't move, please," said the visitor quietly.

"You!" gasped Black.

The tall man with the little pointed beard nodded.

"Keep your hand away from your pocket, colonel," he said; "there is no immediate danger."

He was unarmed. The thin cigar between his white teeth testified his serenity.

"De la Monte!" stammered Black.

Again the bearded man nodded.

"The last time we met was in Cordova," he said, "but you have changed since then."

Black forced a smile.

"You are confusing me with Dr Essley,"

"I am confusing you with Dr Essley," agreed the other. "Yet I think I am justified in my confusion."

He did not remove his cigar, seemed perfectly at ease, even going so far as to cast an eye upon a chair, inviting invitation.

"Essley or Black," he said steadily, "your day is already dusk, and the night is very near."

A cold wave of terror swept over the colonel. He tried to speak, but his throat and his mouth were dry, and he could only make inarticulate noises.

"Tonight – now?" he croaked – his shaking hands went up to his mouth. Yet he was armed and the man before him bore no weapon. A quick movement of his hand and he would lay the spectre which had at one time terrorized Europe. He did not doubt that he was face to face with one of the dreaded Four, and he found himself endeavouring to memorize the face of the man before him for future use. Yet he did not touch the pistol which lay snug in his hip-pocket. He was hypnotized, paralysed by the cool confidence of the other. All that he knew was that he wanted the relief which could only come if this calm man were to go. He felt horribly trapped, saw no way of escape in the presence of this force.

The other divined what was going on in Black's mind.

"I have only one piece of advice to offer you," he said, "and that is this – keep away from the Sandford's dinner."

"Why – why?" stammered Black.

The other walked to the fire-place and flicked the ash of his cigar into the grate.

"Because," he said, without turning round, "at the Sandford dinner you come within the jurisdiction of the 'Four Just Men' – who, as you may know, are a protecting force. Elsewhere – "

"Yes – elsewhere?

"You come within the jurisdiction of the law, Colonel Black, for at this present moment an energetic young Assistant Commissioner of Police is applying for a warrant for your arrest on the charge of murder."

With a little nod, Manfred turned his back and walked leisurely towards the door.

"Stop!"

The words were hissed. Black, revolver in hand, was livid with rage and fear.

Manfred laughed quietly. He did not check his walk, but looked backward over his shoulder.

"Let the cobbler stick to his last," he quoted. "Poison, my dear colonel, is your last – or the knife in the case of Jakobs. An explosion, even of a Webley revolver, would shatter your nerves."

He opened the door and walked out, closing it carefully behind him.

Black sank into the nearest chair, his mouth working, the perspiration streaming down his face.

This was the end. He was a spent force. He crossed the room to the telephone and gave a number. After a little while he got an answer.

Yes, the car was in readiness; there had been no inquiries. He hung up the telephone and called up six depots where cars could be hired. To each he gave the same instructions. Two cars were to be waiting – he changed the locality with each order. Two fast cars, each able to cover the eighty miles to Dover without fear of a breakdown.

"I shall take one," he said, "the other must follow immediately behind – yes, empty. I am going to Dover to meet a party of people."

He would take no risk of a breakdown. The second car must be close at hand in case he had an accident with the first.

He was something of an organizer. In the short space of time he was at the telephone, he arranged the cars so that whatever avenue of escape he was forced to take he would find the vehicles waiting.

This done, he completed his dressing. The reaction from the fear had come. He was filled with black hate for the men who had put a period to his career of villainy. Most of all he hated Sandford, the man who could have saved him.

He would take the risk of the Four – take his chance with the police. Curiously, he feared the police least of all.

One final blow he would strike and break the man whose obstinacy had broken him.

He was mad with anger – he saw nothing but the fulfilment of his plan of revenge. He went into his room, unlocked a cupboard and took out the green bottle. There was no need for the feather, he would do the job thoroughly.

He finished his dressing, pocketed his bank-notes, and slipped the little green bottle into his waistcoat pocket. One last look round he gave, then, with a sense of the old exhilaration which had been his before the arrival of Manfred, he put on his hat, threw an overcoat over his arm and went out.

It was a gay little party that assembled at the Great South Central Hotel. May Sandford had invited a girl friend, and Mr Sandford had brought back the junior partner of one of the City houses he did business with.

Black was late and did not arrive till a quarter of an hour after the time settled for dinner. Sandford had given orders for the meal to be served when the colonel came in.

"Sit down, Black," said Sandford. There was a vacant chair between the ironmaster and his daughter, and into this the colonel dropped.

His hand shook as he took up the spoon to his soup.

He put the spoon down again and unfolded his serviette. A letter dropped out. He knew those grey envelopes now, and crushed the letter into his pocket without attempting to read it.

"Busy man, Black, eh?" smiled Sandford. He was a florid, hearty man with a wisp of white whisker on either side of his rubicund face, and in his pleasant moments he was a very lovable man. "You ought to be grateful I did not agree to the amalgamations – you would have been worked to death."

"Yes," said the colonel shortly. He stuck out his jaw – a trick he had when he was perturbed.

"In a way," bantered the elder man, "you're an admirable chap. If you were a little more reasonable you would be more successful."

"Wouldn't you call me successful?

Sandford pouted thoughtfully.

"Yes and no," he said. "You are not altogether successful. You see, you have achieved what you would call success too easily."

Colonel Black did not pursue the subject, nor did he encourage the other to go any further. He needed opportunity. For a time he had to sit patiently, joining in, with such scraps of speech as he could muster, the conversation that rippled about him.

At his left hand were the girl's wine-glasses. She refused the lighter wines and drew forth a laughing protest from her father.

"Dearie, on your birthday – you must sip some champagne!"

"Champagne, then!" she said gaily. She was happy for many reasons, but principally because – well, just because.

That was the opportunity.

Absent-mindedly he drew her glass nearer, then he found the bottle in his pocket. With one hand he removed the cork and spilt half the contents of the phial on to his serviette. He re-corked the bottle and slipped it into his pocket. He took the glass on to his lap. Twice he wiped the edge of it with the damp napkin. He replaced the glass unnoticed.

Now it was done he felt better. He leant back in his chair, his hands thrust deep into his trousers pockets. It was an inelegant attitude, but he derived a sense of comfort.

"Black, wake up, my dear fellow!" Sandford was talking to him, and he roused himself with a start. "My friend here was rude enough to comment on your hair."

"Eh?" Black put up his hand to his head.

"Oh, it's all right and it isn't disarranged – but how long has it been white?"

"White?"

He had heard of such things and was mildly interested.

"White? Oh – er – quite a time."

He did not further the discussion. The waiters were filling the glasses. He looked across to Sandford. How happy, how self sufficient he was. He intercepted the tender little looks that passed between father and daughter. There was perfect sympathy between the two. It was a pity that in a minute or so one should be dead and the other broken. She so full of life, so splendid of shape, so fresh and lovely. He turned his head and looked at her. Curious, very curious, how frail a thing is life, that a milligram of a colourless fluid should be sufficient to snap the cord that binds soul to body.

The waiter filled the glasses – first the girl's, then his.

He raised his own with unconcern and drank it off.

The girl did not touch hers. She was talking to the man on her left. Black could see only the rounded cheek and one white shoulder.

He waited impatiently.

Sandford tried to bring him into the conversation, but he refused to be drawn. He was content to listen, he said. To listen, to watch and to wait. He saw the slim white fingers close round the stem of the glass, saw her half raise it, still looking towards her partner.

Black pushed his chair a little to one side as the glass reached her lips. She drank, not much, but enough.

The colonel held his breath. She replaced the glass, still talking with the man on her left.

Black counted the slow seconds. He counted sixty – a hundred, oblivious to the fact that Sandford was talking to him.

The drug had failed!

"Are you ill, colonel?"

Everybody was staring at him.

"Ill?" he repeated hoarsely. "No, I am not ill – why should I be ill?"

"Open one of those windows, waiter." A blast of cold air struck him and he shivered.

He left the table hurriedly and went blundering blindly from the room. There was an end to it all.

In the corridor of the hotel he came in his haste into collision with a man. It was the man who had called upon him some time before.

"Excuse me," said the man, catching his arm. "Colonel Black, I believe."

"Stand out of my way." Black spat out the words savagely.

"I am Detective-Sergeant Kay from Scotland Yard, and shall take you into custody."

At the first hint of danger the colonel drew back. Suddenly his fist shot out and caught the officer under the jaw. It was a terrific blow and the detective was unprepared. He went down like a log.

The corridor was empty. Leaving the man upon the floor, the fugitive sped into the lobby. He was hatless, but he shaded his face and passed through the throng in the vestibule into the open air. He signalled a taxi.

"Waterloo, and I will give you a pound if you catch my train."

He was speeding down the Strand in less than a minute. He changed his instructions before the station was reached.

"I have lost the train – drop me at the corner of Eaton Square."

155

At Eaton Square he paid the cabman and dismissed him. With little difficulty he found two closed cars that waited.

"I am Colonel Black," he said, and the first chauffeur touched his cap. "Take the straightest road to Southampton and let the second man follow behind."

The car had not gone far before he changed his mind.

"Go first to the Junior Turf Club in Pall Mall," he said.

Arrived at the club, he beckoned the porter. "Tell Sir Isaac Tramber that he is wanted at once," he directed.

Ikey was in the club – it was a chance shot of the colonel's, but it bagged his man.

"Get your coat and hat," said Black hurriedly to the flustered baronet.

"But – "

"No buts," snarled the other savagely. "Get your coat and hat, unless you want to be hauled out of your club to the nearest police station."

Reluctantly Ikey went back to the club and returned in a few seconds struggling into his great-coat.

"Now what the devil is this all about?" he demanded peevishly; then, as the light of a street lamp caught the colonel's uncovered head, he gasped:

"Good Lord! Your hair has gone white! You look just like that fellow Essley!"

JUSTICE

"Where are we going?" asked Sir Isaac faintly.

"We are going to Southampton," growled Black in his ear. "We shall find some friends there." He grinned in the darkness. Then, leaning forward, he gave instructions in a low tone to the chauffeur.

The car jerked forward and in a few minutes it had crossed Hammersmith Broadway and was speeding towards Barnes.

Scarcely had it cleared the traffic when a long grey racing car cut perilously across the crowded space, dodging with extraordinary agility a number of vehicles, and, unheeding the caustic comments of the drivers, it went on in the same direction as Black's car had taken.

He had cleared Kingston and was on the Sandown road when he heard the loud purring of a car behind. He turned and looked, expecting to find his second car, but a punctured tyre held Black's reserve on Putney Heath. Black was a little uneasy, though it was no unusual thing for cars to travel the main Portsmouth road at that hour of the night.

He knew, too, that he could not hope to keep ahead of his pursuer. He caught the unmistakable sound which accompanies the racing car in motion.

"We'll wait till the road gets a little broader," he said, "and then we'll let that chap pass us."

He conveyed the gist of this intention to the chauffeur.

The car behind showed no disposition to go ahead until Sandown and Cobham had been left behind and the lights of Guildford were almost in sight.

Then, on a lonely stretch of road, two miles from the town, the car, without any perceptible effort, shot level with them and then drew ahead on the offside. Then it slowed, and the touring car had perforce to follow its example.

Black watched the manoeuvre with some misgiving. Slower and slower went the racing car till it stopped crossways in the road; it stopped, too, in a position which made it impossible for the touring car to pass.

Black's man drew up with a jerk.

They saw, by the light of their lamps, two men get out of the motor ahead and make what seemed to be a cursory examination of a wheel. Then one walked back, slowly and casually, till he came to where Black and his companion sat.

"Excuse me," said the stranger, "I think I know you."

Of a sudden an electric lamp flashed in Black's face. More to the point, in the spreading rays of the light, clear to be seen was the nickel-plated barrel of a revolver, and it was pointed straight at Black.

"You will alight, Mr Black – you and your companion," said the unknown calmly.

In the bright light that flooded him, Black could make no move. Without a word he stepped down on to the roadway, his companion following him.

"Go ahead," said the man with the revolver.

The two obeyed. Another flood of light met them. The driver of the first car was standing up, electric torch in one hand, revolver in the other. He directed them curtly to enter the tonneau. The first of their captors turned to give directions to the chauffeur of the grey touring car, then he sprang into the body in which they sat and took a seat opposite them.

"Put your hands on your knees," he commanded, as his little lamp played over them.

Black brought his gloved hands forward reluctantly. Sir Isaac, half dead with fright, followed his example.

The car moved forward. Their warder, concentrating his lamp upon their knees, kept watch while his companion drove the car forward at a racing pace.

They struck off from the main road and took a narrow country lane which was unfamiliar to Black, and for ten minutes they twisted and turned in what seemed the heart of the country. Then they stopped.

"Get down," ordered the man with the lamp.

Neither Black nor his friend had spoken one word up till now.

"What is the game?" asked Black.

"Get down," commanded the other. With a curse, the big man descended.

There were two other men waiting for them.

"I suppose this is the 'Four Just Men' farce," said Black with a sneer.

"That you shall learn," said one of those who were waiting.

They were conducted by a long, rough path through a field, through a little copse, until ahead of them in the night loomed a small building.

It was in darkness. It gave Black the impression of being a chapel. He had little time to take any note of its construction. He heard Sir Isaac's quick breathing behind him and the snick of a lock. The hand that held his arm now relaxed.

"Stay where you are," said a voice.

Black waited. There was growing in his heart a sickly fear of what all this signified.

"Step forward," said a voice.

Black moved two steps forward and suddenly the big room in which he stood blazed with light. He raised his hand to veil his eyes from the dazzling glow.

The sight he saw was a remarkable one. He was in a chapel; he saw the stained glass windows, but in place of the altar there was a low platform which ran along one end of the building.

It was draped with black and set with three desks. It reminded him of nothing so much as a judge's desk, save that the hangings were of purple, the desks of black oak, and the carpet that covered the dais of the same sombre hue.

Three men sat at the desks. They were masked, and a diamond pin in the cravat of one glittered in the light of the huge electrolier which hung from the vaulted roof. Gonsalez had a weakness for jewels.

The remaining member of the Four was to the right of the prisoners.

With the stained-glass windows, the raftered roof, and the solemn character of the architecture, the illusion of the chapel ended. There was no other furniture on the floor; it was tiled and bare of chair or pew.

Black took all this in quickly. He noted a door behind the three, through which they came and apparently made their exit. He could see no means of escape save by the way he had come.

The central figure of the three at the desk spoke in a voice which was harsh and stern and uncompromising.

"Morris Black," he said solemnly, "what of Fanks?"

Black shrugged his shoulders and looked round as though weary of a question which he found it impossible to answer.

"What of Jakobs, of Coleman, of a dozen men who have stood in your way and have died?" asked the voice.

Still Black was silent.

His eye took in the situation. Behind him were two doors, and he observed that the key was in the lock. He could see that he was in an old Norman chapel which private enterprise had restored for a purpose.

The door was modern and of the usual "churchy" type.

"Isaac Tramber," said Number One, "what part have you played?"

"I don't know," stammered Sir Isaac, "I am as much in the dark as you are. I think the bucket shop idea is perfectly beastly. Now look here, is there anything else I can tell you, because I am most anxious to get out of this affair with clean hands?"

He made a step forward and Black reached out a hand to restrain him, but was pulled back by the man at his side.

"Come here," said Number One. His knees shaking under him, Sir Isaac walked quickly up the aisle floor.

"I'll do anything I can," he said eagerly, as he stood like a penitent boy before the master's figure. "Any information I can give you I shall be most happy to give."

"Stop!" roared Black. His face was livid with rage. "Stop," he said hoarsely, "you don't know what you're doing, Ikey. Keep your mouth shut and stand by me and you'll not suffer."

"There is only one thing I know," Sir Isaac went on, "and that is that Black had a bit of a row with Fanks – "

The words were scarcely out of his mouth when three shots rang out in rapid succession. The Four had not attempted to disarm Black. With lightning-like rapidity he had whipped out his Browning pistol and had fired at the traitor.

In a second he was at the door. An instant later the key was turned and he was through.

"Shoot – shoot, Manfred," said a voice from the dais. But they were too late – Black had vanished into the darkness. As the two men sprang after him, they stood for a moment silhouetted against the light from the chapel within.

"Crack! crack!" A nickel bullet struck the stone supports of the doorway and covered them with fine dust and splinters of stone.

"Put the lights out and follow," said Manfred quickly.

He was too late, for Black had a start, and the fear and hatred in him lent him unsuspected speed.

The brute instinct in him led him across the field unerringly. He reached the tiny road, turned to the left, and found the grey racing car waiting, unattended.

He sprang to the crank and turned it. He was in the driver's seat in an instant. He had to take risks – there might be ditches on either side of the road, but he turned the wheel over till it almost locked and brought his foot down over the pedal.

The car jumped forward, lurched to the side, recovered itself, and went bumping and crashing along the road.

"It's no good," said Manfred. He saw the tail-lights of the car disappearing. "Let's get back."

He had slipped off his mask.

They raced back to the chapel. The lights were on again. Sir Isaac Tramber lay stone-dead on the floor. The bullet had struck him in the left shoulder and had passed through his heart.

But it was not to him they looked. Number One lay still and motionless on the floor in a pool of blood.

"Look to the injury," he said, "and unless it is fatal do not unmask me."

Poiccart and Gonsalez made a brief examination of the wound.

"It's pretty serious."

In this terse sentence they summarized their judgement.

"I thought it was," said the wounded man quietly. "You had better get on to Southampton. He'll probably pick up Fellowe" – he smiled through his mask – "I suppose I ought to call him Lord Francis Ledborough now. He's a nephew of mine and a sort of a police-commissioner himself. I wired him to follow me. You might pick up his car and go on together. Manfred can stay with me. Take this mask off."

Gonsalez stooped down and gently removed the silk half-mask. Then he started back.

"Lord Verlond," he exclaimed with surprise, and Manfred, who knew, nodded.

The road was clear of traffic at this hour of the night. It was dark and none too wide in places for a man who had not touched the steering-wheel of a car for some years, but Black, bareheaded, sat and drove the big machine ahead without fear of consequences. Once he went rocking through a little town at racing speed.

A policeman who attempted to hold him up narrowly escaped with his life. Black reached open road again with no injury save a shattered mud-guard that had caught a lamp-post on a sharp turn. He went through Winchester at top speed – again there was an attempt to stop him. Two big wagons had been drawn up in the main street, but he saw them in time and took a side turning, and cleared town again more by good luck than otherwise. He knew now that his flight was known to the police. He must change his plans. He admitted to himself that he had few plans to change: he had arranged to leave England by one of two ports, Dover or Southampton.

He had hoped to reach the Le Havre boat without attracting attention, but that was now out of the question. The boats would be watched, and he had no disguise which would help him.

Eight miles south of Winchester he overtook another car and passed it before he realized that this must be the second car he had hired. With the realization came two reports – the front tyres of his car had punctured.

His foot pressed on the brake and he slowed the car to a standstill.

Here was luck! To come to grief at the very spot where his relief was at hand!

He jumped out of the car and stood revealed in the glare of the lamps of the oncoming car, his arms outstretched.

The car drew up within a few feet of him. "Take me on to Southampton; I have broken down," he said, and the chauffeur said something unintelligible.

Black opened the door of the car and stepped in. The door slammed behind him before he was aware that there were other occupants.

"Who – ?" he began.

Then two hands seized him, something cold and hard snapped on his wrists, and a familiar voice said:

"I am Lord Francis Ledborough, an assistant commissioner of police, and I shall take you into custody on a charge of wilful murder."

"Ledborough?" repeated Black dully.

"You know me best as Constable Fellowe," said the voice.

Black was hanged at Pentonville gaol on the 27th of March, 19– , and Lord Francis Ledborough, sitting by the side of an invalid uncle's bed, read such meagre descriptions as were given to the press.

"Did you know him, sir?" he asked.

The old earl turned fretfully.

"Know him?" he snarled. "Of course I knew him; he is the only friend of mine that has ever been hanged."

"Where did you meet him?" persisted a sceptical AC of Police.

"I never met him," said the old man grimly, "he met me."

And he made a little grimace, for the wound in his shoulder was still painful.

Edgar Wallace

Big Foot

Footprints and a dead woman bring together Superintendent Minton and the amateur sleuth Mr Cardew. Who is the man in the shrubbery? Who is the singer of the haunting Moorish tune? Why is Hannah Shaw so determined to go to Pawsy, 'a dog lonely place' she had previously detested? Death lurks in the dark and someone must solve the mystery before BIG FOOT strikes again, in a yet more fiendish manner.

Bones In London

The new Managing Director of Schemes Ltd has an elegant London office and a theatrically dressed assistant – however, Bones, as he is better known, is bored. Luckily there is a slump in the shipping market and it is not long before Joe and Fred Pole pay Bones a visit. They are totally unprepared for Bones' unnerving style of doing business, unprepared for his unique style of innocent and endearing mischief.

EDGAR WALLACE

BONES OF THE RIVER

'Taking the little paper from the pigeon's leg, Hamilton saw it was from Sanders and marked URGENT. *Send Bones instantly to Lujamalababa… Arrest and bring to headquarters the witch doctor.*'

It is a time when the world's most powerful nations are vying for colonial honour, a time of trading steamers and tribal chiefs. In the mysterious African territories administered by Commissioner Sanders, Bones persistently manages to create his own unique style of innocent and endearing mischief.

THE DAFFODIL MYSTERY

When Mr Thomas Lyne, poet, poseur and owner of Lyne's Emporium insults a cashier, Odette Rider, she resigns. Having summoned detective Jack Tarling to investigate another employee, Mr Milburgh, Lyne now changes his plans. Tarling and his Chinese companion refuse to become involved. They pay a visit to Odette's flat and in the hall Tarling meets Sam, convicted felon and protégé of Lyne. Next morning Tarling discovers a body. The hands are crossed on the breast, adorned with a handful of daffodils.

EDGAR WALLACE

THE JOKER
(USA: THE COLOSSUS)

While the millionaire Stratford Harlow is in Princetown, not only does he meet with his lawyer Mr Ellenbury but he gets his first glimpse of the beautiful Aileen Rivers, niece of the actor and convicted felon Arthur Ingle. When Aileen is involved in a car accident on the Thames Embankment, the driver is James Carlton of Scotland Yard. Later that evening Carlton gets a call. It is Aileen. She needs help.

THE SQUARE EMERALD
(USA: THE GIRL FROM SCOTLAND YARD)

'Suicide on the left,' says Chief Inspector Coldwell pleasantly, as he and Leslie Maughan stride along the Thames Embankment during a brutally cold night. A gaunt figure is sprawled across the parapet. But Coldwell soon discovers that Peter Dawlish, fresh out of prison for forgery, is not considering suicide but murder. Coldwell suspects Druze as the intended victim. Maughan disagrees. If Druze dies, she says, 'It will be because he does not love children!'

OTHER TITLES BY EDGAR WALLACE AVAILABLE DIRECT
FROM HOUSE OF STRATUS

Quantity	£	$(US)	$(CAN)	€
THE ADMIRABLE CARFEW	6.99	12.95	19.95	13.50
THE ANGEL OF TERROR	6.99	12.95	19.95	13.50
THE AVENGER (USA: THE HAIRY ARM)	6.99	12.95	19.95	13.50
BARBARA ON HER OWN	6.99	12.95	19.95	13.50
BIG FOOT	6.99	12.95	19.95	13.50
THE BLACK ABBOT	6.99	12.95	19.95	13.50
BONES	6.99	12.95	19.95	13.50
BONES IN LONDON	6.99	12.95	19.95	13.50
BONES OF THE RIVER	6.99	12.95	19.95	13.50
THE CLUE OF THE NEW PIN	6.99	12.95	19.95	13.50
THE CLUE OF THE SILVER KEY	6.99	12.95	19.95	13.50
THE CLUE OF THE TWISTED CANDLE	6.99	12.95	19.95	13.50
THE COAT OF ARMS				
(USA: THE ARRANWAYS MYSTERY)	6.99	12.95	19.95	13.50
THE COUNCIL OF JUSTICE	6.99	12.95	19.95	13.50
THE CRIMSON CIRCLE	6.99	12.95	19.95	13.50
THE DAFFODIL MYSTERY	6.99	12.95	19.95	13.50
THE DARK EYES OF LONDON				
(USA: THE CROAKERS)	6.99	12.95	19.95	13.50
THE DAUGHTERS OF THE NIGHT	6.99	12.95	19.95	13.50
A DEBT DISCHARGED	6.99	12.95	19.95	13.50
THE DEVIL MAN	6.99	12.95	19.95	13.50
THE DOOR WITH SEVEN LOCKS	6.99	12.95	19.95	13.50
THE DUKE IN THE SUBURBS	6.99	12.95	19.95	13.50
THE FACE IN THE NIGHT	6.99	12.95	19.95	13.50
THE FEATHERED SERPENT	6.99	12.95	19.95	13.50
THE FLYING SQUAD	6.99	12.95	19.95	13.50
THE FORGER (USA: THE CLEVER ONE)	6.99	12.95	19.95	13.50
THE FOUR JUST MEN	6.99	12.95	19.95	13.50
FOUR SQUARE JANE	6.99	12.95	19.95	13.50

ALL HOUSE OF STRATUS BOOKS ARE AVAILABLE FROM GOOD BOOKSHOPS
OR DIRECT FROM THE PUBLISHER:

Internet: www.houseofstratus.com including synopses and features.

Email: sales@houseofstratus.com
info@houseofstratus.com
(please quote author, title and credit card details.)

OTHER TITLES BY EDGAR WALLACE AVAILABLE DIRECT
FROM HOUSE OF STRATUS

Quantity		£	$(US)	$(CAN)	€
☐	THE FOURTH PLAGUE	6.99	12.95	19.95	13.50
☐	THE FRIGHTENED LADY	6.99	12.95	19.95	13.50
☐	GOOD EVANS	6.99	12.95	19.95	13.50
☐	THE HAND OF POWER	6.99	12.95	19.95	13.50
☐	THE IRON GRIP	6.99	12.95	19.95	13.50
☐	THE JOKER (USA: THE COLOSSUS)	6.99	12.95	19.95	13.50
☐	THE KEEPERS OF THE KING'S PEACE	6.99	12.95	19.95	13.50
☐	THE LAW OF THE FOUR JUST MEN	6.99	12.95	19.95	13.50
☐	THE LONE HOUSE MYSTERY	6.99	12.95	19.95	13.50
☐	THE MAN WHO BOUGHT LONDON	6.99	12.95	19.95	13.50
☐	THE MAN WHO KNEW	6.99	12.95	19.95	13.50
☐	THE MAN WHO WAS NOBODY	6.99	12.95	19.95	13.50
☐	THE MIND OF MR J G REEDER				
	(USA: THE MURDER BOOK OF J G REEDER)	6.99	12.95	19.95	13.50
☐	MORE EDUCATED EVANS	6.99	12.95	19.95	13.50
☐	MR J G REEDER RETURNS				
	(USA: MR REEDER RETURNS)	6.99	12.95	19.95	13.50
☐	MR JUSTICE MAXELL	6.99	12.95	19.95	13.50
☐	RED ACES	6.99	12.95	19.95	13.50
☐	ROOM 13	6.99	12.95	19.95	13.50
☐	SANDERS	6.99	12.95	19.95	13.50
☐	SANDERS OF THE RIVER	6.99	12.95	19.95	13.50
☐	THE SINISTER MAN	6.99	12.95	19.95	13.50
☐	THE SQUARE EMERALD				
	(USA: THE GIRL FROM SCOTLAND YARD)	6.99	12.95	19.95	13.50
☐	THE THREE JUST MEN	6.99	12.95	19.95	13.50
☐	THE THREE OAK MYSTERY	6.99	12.95	19.95	13.50
☐	THE TRAITOR'S GATE	6.99	12.95	19.95	13.50
☐	WHEN THE GANGS CAME TO LONDON	6.99	12.95	19.95	13.50

Tel: Order Line
         0800 169 1780 (UK)
          800 724 1100 (USA)
         International
         +44 (0) 1845 527700 (UK)
         +01   845 463 1100 (USA)

Fax: +44 (0) 1845 527711 (UK)
         +01   845 463 0018 (USA)
         (please quote author, title and credit card details.)

Send to: **House of Stratus Sales Department**
         Thirsk Industrial Park
         York Road, Thirsk
         North Yorkshire, YO7 3BX
         UK

PAYMENT

Please tick currency you wish to use:

☐ £ (Sterling)   ☐ $ (US)   ☐ $ (CAN)   ☐ € (Euros)

Allow for shipping costs charged per order plus an amount per book as set out in the tables below:

CURRENCY/DESTINATION

	£(Sterling)	$(US)	$(CAN)	€ (Euros)
Cost per order				
UK	1.50	2.25	3.50	2.50
Europe	3.00	4.50	6.75	5.00
North America	3.00	3.50	5.25	5.00
Rest of World	3.00	4.50	6.75	5.00
Additional cost per book				
UK	0.50	0.75	1.15	0.85
Europe	1.00	1.50	2.25	1.70
North America	1.00	1.00	1.50	1.70
Rest of World	1.50	2.25	3.50	3.00

PLEASE SEND CHEQUE OR INTERNATIONAL MONEY ORDER
payable to: HOUSE OF STRATUS LTD or HOUSE OF STRATUS INC. or card payment as indicated

STERLING EXAMPLE

Cost of book(s):..................... Example: 3 x books at £6.99 each: £20.97
Cost of order: .... Example: £1.50 (Delivery to UK address)
Additional cost per book:.............. Example: 3 x £0.50: £1.50
Order total including shipping:........... Example: £23.97

VISA, MASTERCARD, SWITCH, AMEX:

☐ ☐ ☐ ☐ ☐ ☐ ☐ ☐ ☐ ☐ ☐ ☐ ☐ ☐ ☐ ☐ ☐ ☐

Issue number (Switch only):

☐ ☐ ☐

Start Date: **Expiry Date:**

☐ ☐ / ☐ ☐   ☐ ☐ / ☐ ☐

Signature: _____

NAME: _____

ADDRESS: _____

COUNTRY: _____

ZIP/POSTCODE: _____

Please allow 28 days for delivery. Despatch normally within 48 hours.

Prices subject to change without notice.
Please tick box if you do not wish to receive any additional information. ☐

House of Stratus publishes many other titles in this genre; please check our website (**www.houseofstratus.com**) for more details.